The Last Hour

ACW Press
5501 N. 7th Ave. #502
Phoenix, AZ 85013

Cover design by Eric Walljasper
Page design by Steven R. Laube
Typeset using Electra 12pt. Designed in 1935 by William Addision Dwiggins, Electra has been a standard book typeface since its release because of its evenness of design and high legibility.

Publisher's Cataloging-in-Publication
(Provided by Quality Books, Inc.)

Young, Kim.
The Last Hour: a Novel / Kim Young -- 1st ed.
p. cm.
ISBN 0-9656749-1-6

1. Eschatology--Fiction. I. Title

PS3575.Y68L37 1997 [Fic]
QBI97-40705

Printed in the United States of America

To obtain more copies please contact:
The Vantage Group
Dick Sleeper Distribution
1830 Air Lane Drive Suite 3-B
Nashville, TN 37210-3817
1-800-699-9911 ext. 150
Fax: 615-889-1439

Dedicated in loving memory of our beloved,
SAPD Officer Fabian Dale Dominguez,
brutally killed in the line of duty,
and whose death brings home
2 Timothy 3:1.

"This know also, that in the last days perilous times
shall come. For men shall be lovers of themselves,
covetous, boasters, proud, blasphemers,
disobedient to parents, ungrateful, unholy,
Without natural affection, unforgiving,
slanderous, without self-control, brutal,
despisers of those that are good,
Traitors, rash, conceited, lovers of
pleasures more than lovers of God."

Kim Young is a Th.M student at Dallas Theological Seminary and has studied Biblical prophecy for many years. She has a B.A. in Journalism from Texas Tech University, a Texas Real Estate Brokers License, and has been a Precept Upon Precept Inductive Bible study leader. Young lives in San Antonio, Texas with her husband and four children. She has been published in numerous periodicals.

I wish to express my sincere gratitude to the
following people who assisted me with their time,
energy, encouragement and knowledge:
Richard Bohrer, Kelly Young,
Thelma Harvey, Dode Harvey,
Paul Brake, Dr. Michael Fanning,
Molly Harvey, Charlotte Mitchell
and Steve Laube.

FOREWORD

As I continue to study end times prophecy, I've come to the realization that we can't be dogmatic that these events will happen before or after the rapture. Every day I see things that make me wonder if the seals are being broken. Regardless, I can't help but believe they are only a short time away.

Scripture teaches that there will be a seven-year period in which God deals with Israel. No one knows the time Jesus will come for His bride, and I don't presume to guarantee that it occurs any earlier than before the Great Tribulation–sometime during the last 3-1/2 years. Are you ready?

Whether or not Christians are raptured before, during, or after God's wrath, we are to be about the work of His Kingdom. There will come a day of reckoning when every person will be called before God. Some to everlasting peace and others to eternal fire.

Prologue

The noonday sun beamed brightly through the large windows of Ford Devoe's eighty-fifth-floor penthouse office. The traffic and pedestrians far below looked more like an army of sugar ants raiding a discarded chocolate bar. Rarely did Ford venture out in the crowds, preferring instead the safe comfortable sanctuary of his own kingdom.

Today he had ordered lunch in, not even wanting to subject himself to the corporate dining room one floor below. Not satisfied listening to his own thoughts and not willing to fight the silence, Devoe turned on the radio.

Oh, that's just great! Josh Cohen! It would be that time of day. He left the radio on long enough for Josh to launch into a long monologue about the evils of Ford Devoe.

Devoe turned off the radio and cursed. *Why do I listen to that garbage? He makes me furious! I've got to stop that pile of manure from spreading his stink any further. Who do I know in the FCC?*

He stared out the window. The latest copy of *American Entrepreneur* lay on his desk with his picture big as life on the cover.

How dare Cohen question my motives in returning the political process back to the people. There's more talent and power in my little finger than he'll ever dream of hoping for.

Devoe turned around to grab the magazine, stopping momentarily to stare at the telephone. *I need someone to tell my side of the story.*

Devoe hit the voice dial button of his phone. "1-800-444-Chat." The phone stopped dialing after the 444. "Good grief!" Devoe cursed out loud. *What is that number?* "2428."

Devoe listened as the phone automatically dialed the Josh Cohen Show. He jumped when he heard a familiar voice on the other end.

"Hello, you're on the Josh Cohen show. This is Josh Cohen."

Devoe nearly hung the phone up as he grabbed the receiver.

"Uh... yes,... uh, my name is John... I'd like to speak with Mr. Cohen about his negative portrayal of Ford Devoe."

"In the flesh. My call screener just rushed to the loo, leaving me high and dry. Somebody has to do the job. I'm not too bad at answering the phone myself."

Devoe's hand began to shake.

This was a mistake! As he began to speak he fought to control the high-pitched nasal sound his voice coach had warned him of.

"Yes, well, Mr. Cohen, you are all wrong about Ford Devoe."

"Oh, you know him personally?"

"We're old friends. Bunkmates in boot camp our first year at the Service Academy."

"So, you know the little general intimately."

"You could say that." Devoe had to control a snicker.

"Tell me about him. What have I said that's wrong about Mr. Devoe. I'll be the first to admit a mistake. Shoot!"

"First, he's one of the most brilliant minds our country has ever known. He's focused, in control, and a man of action. The army made a grave mistake in not recognizing his genius. Just look at what he has accomplished. Going from lowly salesman to the owner, president, and CEO of the world's largest computer security system. His advice and expertise are sought by global leaders and international policy-makers."

Josh began to chuckle. "You sound like his greatest fan. What was your name again?"

Devoe stuttered. "Uh,... Sam, Sam...from...from Beaumont."

Josh roared his delight. "Now, which is it, John or Sam? Or is it possible we have the little general himself on the phone? No wonder you sound like his greatest fan. You are your own greatest fan. Honestly, do you think we wouldn't recognize your voice? Every stand-up comedian in the country is doing your act."

"That's a lie! I'm not– "

Josh interrupted, "We'll be sending you an audio of this call. Thank you for being on the air."

Devoe slammed down the receiver. "He'll pay! He'll pay!"

1

"So will I make my holy name known in the midst of my people Israel; and I will not let them pollute my holy name any more; and the heathen shall know that I am the Lord, the Holy One in Israel."
(Ezekiel 39:7)

Greetings chit-chatters across the globe. This is Josh Cohen and the DIA Network. Call me at 1-800-444-CHAT. We'll send an audio of our conversation to those of you who call in.

"Prepare yourselves, because I'm mad. I'm really mad today, folks.

"Republicans and Democrats alike are not following through with the wishes of the American people.

"And I'm real tired of people thinking Ford Devoe's American Party is anything but a slick ad campaign designed to throw a wrench into the two-party process.

"Taxes, welfare, Medicaid, immigration, foreign policy, and the list goes on. Instead of real change, it's politics as usual, and I'm tired of it.

"I'm tired of sitting here day after day, educating the public, making a difference at election time, and then having to put up with weak politicians afraid of upsetting the status quo.

"Quite honestly, I'm tired of listening to the President's skillfully crafted lies.

"I'm tired of the press, when they know through Gallup polls what the public is thinking, slanting the news in the opposite direction and expecting us to buy it.

"I'm tired of skewered laws that protect the criminal and malign law enforcement, and I'm not talking about brute force or unconstitutional use of power." Josh slammed his fist down on the desk and his voice grew louder.

"I'm talking about how honest, law-abiding people doing an honest day's work have to bend to political correctness. How nowadays no one takes responsibility for his actions, choosing instead to blame his background.

"I'm tired of it, folks, really tired of it. And I intend to do something about it. Back in a minute."

What a day! Josh grabbed a diet Coke out of the refrigerator, collapsed on the roomy sofa, and reached for the remote control. He looked at his watch, 5:00 p.m.

Hum, home early today. Time to watch what most people call the news. He dreaded another dinner with another new advertiser.

This is getting old.

He closed his eyes.

The monumental growth of his radio show, "Democracy in Action," remained an enigma. No one dreamed he would experience a huge success and revive talk radio as a major media form to be reckoned with.

Life was a dream. Fame, power, money—he could go anywhere and do anything. What a difference six years had made. From a medium market, West Coast afternoon drive time, divorced radio announcer, to the East Coast, syndication on 660 plus stations, 30 million listeners, and one of the nation's most eligible bachelors. Josh Cohen, the giant of talk radio.

Josh thought of his two ex-wives and chuckled. The theme song for Carnival Cruise Lines popped into his mind, "If they could see me now..." *Good thing alimony's not retroactive.* He snorted. The mention of Israel drew his attention across the room to the large screen Sony.

"This is Tom Donnelly. We now break to our correspondent in Israel... Irene, what is the talk in Israel?"

"Tom, the Knesset has not issued a formal statement other than to say they are standing by the treaties they've signed with the governments of Saudi Arabia, Egypt, Syria, Jordan, and the PLO. But our sources indicate there has been some troop movement on the Syrian and Lebanon border," she explained.

"What's causing this activity?" he asked.

"Tom, what I can gather from key Palestinians, there is an underground movement, possibly world-wide, by the Muslims to retake Jerusalem. As you know from recent talks between Israel and the PLO, Israel has adamantly refused to consider making Jerusalem an international city. And to make matters worse, the mayor in Jerusalem has been in the news a lot lately vowing to uphold the Jerusalem Covenant at any cost.

"It has been suggested by the mayor's critics that, in part, this uprising against Israel is due to the plans for the millennia celebration of King David's declaration of Jerusalem as the capital of the Jewish commonwealth."

She swept her hair from her face and continued. "As to actions being taken to get this small, but mighty country ready for an attack, Tom, Israel has issued an emergency evacuation of all public buildings. And, of course, the military is on full alert."

"Irene, that sounds serious."

"Yes, Tom. However, the atmosphere here in Jerusalem is one of guarded concern, much like it was when Iraq sent sorties flying over Jerusalem in 1990. The majority of people are still going about their daily business preparing for the Feast of Trumpets, which begins next week. I don't think we'll see war preparations from the everyday folks here unless bombs are actually exploded in the area.

"Thank you, Irene. Now we'll go to James Minter, our Washington correspondent. James, what is the reaction from the White House?"

"Tom, this is the first time in my career that the White House has not immediately issued a statement supporting Israel in response to a national threat."

"James, what do you attribute this silence to?"

"Well, Tom, the recent harassment charges against the president by Debra Thames has caused quite a rift between the President and First Lady, and they've been unable to come to a consensus regarding the United States friendship with Israel and how we should respond."

"Uh...James, did I hear you correctly?"

"Yes, Tom, I'm fully aware of the implications. But I'm here with reporters from around the country, and everyone seems to agree that, to date, this is the worst breakdown of Presidential leadership we've witnessed."

"Thank you, James. We'll get back to you as the news breaks. We now return you to your local stations."

The gray morning mist hung low over Jerusalem and should have been an ominous sign to Itzak as he hurried to his office. The early call from the deputy of defense had produced a heaviness in his chest.

He knew the recent lull in terrorist activity was temporary at best. And though Israel's leaders walked on egg shells, not wanting to offend the global community, Israelites on the whole had ignored all the warning signs.

"Prime Minister," his secretary said through the intercom as he took off his hat and coat, "Deputy of Defense Lieberman and Foreign Affairs Minister Sadle are here to see you."

"Send them in."

Itzak directed the men toward the conference table. Deep lines etched his brow, bringing white hair closer to bushy gray eyebrows, threatening to erase the small space between his dark eyes.

Deputy Defense Minister Lieberman spread a large map of the region across the conference table. He removed a red pen from the pocket of his white shirt and pointed to the UN zone, separating Syria from the Golan Heights, and the nine-mile-deep Israeli Security Zone that separated her from Lebanon. "Our systems analysis operator at DCI, in Houston, Texas, called this morning insisting we look at last night's satellite imaging reconnaissance photos," Lieberman said.

Those words caused Itzak's chest to tighten. *Not yet, please, God, not yet.*

"They reveal a build-up of machinery in these two areas." He drew bold red circles on the map. "Those photos also reveal movement out of Egypt, Turkey, and the southern Russian states."

Itzak searched the stone faces of his cabinet members. He pulled out a handkerchief and wiped his brow. "What are your opinions?"

Defense Minister Lieberman pulled over a chair and sat down. "The United States got us into this mess. Let them get us out."

"Have you lost your mind?" Sadle threw up his hands. "Do you honestly think the United States has any intention of insuring Jerusalem remains in the hands of Jews? They're just waiting for an opportunity to get us before the United Nations and make their case for an international city."

"You know, gentlemen," Itzak began, "if, as the Mossad suggests, Saudi Arabia is militarily involved with Syria, then relying on an Arab Peace Treaty is useless."

Sadle's face contorted in anger. "So what are you saying, Itzak, that this is all my fault? Do you think the Foreign Affairs Department is to blame for your land-for-peace deals? Ever since

I got the glory for bringing all the parties together, you've held a grudge against me." The windows vibrated with his ear-piercing shouts.

"Come on, you two." Lieberman stepped between the men. He held little respect for either, having gained access to the files containing their most intimate secrets.

The three men stood momentarily lost in individual thoughts. The heat of the moment subsided, and Itzak dropped into a chair. "Years of negotiations–land deals–all for nothing."

In those brief moments, Itzak could hear in his head the hostile protests of orthodox Jews–protests that were now clearly prophetic warnings against land for peace.

"We have no choice. We must prepare for war, gentlemen." Itzak bowed his head.

Tom Donnelly sauntered out of the makeup room adjusting his maroon silk tie. He dreaded the debate he would moderate that evening between the president and Ford Devoe. Any other time he would look forward to making one or the other look a fool in front of his millions of viewers.

A heaviness gripped his chest. If he had been a superstitious man, he might have mentioned his sense of foreboding to one of the passing cameramen.

"Hey, Tom, looking forward to a great show tonight."

He forced himself to smile and give a half-hearted salute in response.

What's bugging me?

He struggled to find an answer before his guests arrived.

Is it Devoe? That strange little arrogant man with a big stupid grin. Speaking of the devil.

Tom looked up to see Devoe walk into the studio.

Bodacious fool.

He couldn't help but remember the billionaire's bizarre media blitz several years ago that celebrated the beheading of a radical Muslim fundamentalist after one of Devoe's security compounds in Saudi Arabia was bombed during an Islamic uprising.

Some national hero. Why was I the lucky stooge who launched his global popularity?

Donnelly cursed himself.

And here I am promoting the jerk again. Giving him a soapbox to launch his latest public relations ploy--fighting the huge expansion of government. What a joke. He's an expansion of government all to himself. The righter of all wrongs. Give me a break!

He ran his hand through his thick brown hair.

I can't believe that idiot actually thinks he's a national leader, a savior of the common man. And here I'm giving him the power and recognition he craves.

He cursed again. Donnelly knew Devoe had arranged this debate to discredit Bob Wells and stop the current push in the Senate to ratify the United Nation's monetary policies.

He read his notes to himself–*The public is deeply divided over a world monetary system. Congressional leadership has given President Wells the votes he needs to ratify the monetary treaty. Public outcry has held it up in the Senate. Ask what each one wants to do about that?*

He wrinkled his face trying to decide what questions would generate the biggest fight on the air.

Let's see. Devoe is going to rally around the various Christian ministries and right-wing organizations that proclaimed a connection between the previous and current Presidents, the Council on Foreign Relations and the Trilateral Commission, claiming NAFTA, GATT, and WTO all had their roots there and that a world currency would lead to a devaluation of the dollar.

I know Devoe thinks Christians are kooks and their message gobbledygook. How can I get that out of him?

Donnelly pulled out the small bottle of pills and headed for a water fountain. Seeing a messenger running toward him with a portable phone, he poured out one more pill than was necessary.

"Mr. Donnelly," the messenger said, taking a deep breath, "it's the White House calling."

"Donnelly, here."

"Tom, this is Emily." Her voice oozed with sweetness.

"Well, if this isn't my lucky day. How do I rate a call from the First Lady?"

"Oh, Tom, stop kidding around. You said we'd get together soon. Why haven't you called?"

He could picture her pouty red lips close to the receiver. "I'll try to make an excuse tomorrow and stop by the White House. Tell the security at the gate to put me on the visitation list."

"Tom...I was hoping you might come by tonight."

He enjoyed hearing her beg. "Emily, you know I've got the debate tonight."

"I know, but Bob will be out till the early hours of the morning going over every word spoken during that debate. Pleaasse. I really need to see you."

"Okay, okay, Emily." His resistance grew weak.

"Hurrah! And do me another favor, Tom. Cream Devoe tonight. I really hate that guy."

"Oh, come on, Emily, you don't hate him. After all, if it hadn't been for him, Bob might not be president at all."

"Yeah, well, if it's up to him, we might not be here next year either."

"I'll do my best, Emily. Thanks for the call. I've gotta go." Tom hung up the phone. His prospects for the evening were looking up.

So why doesn't it feel that way?

Pope Simon Peter II spent his first days at the Vatican in seclusion writing his papal encyclical and contemplating the changes he would introduce in the church. He kept his office dark except for the dainty lamp casting out its rose-tinted circular light over the sheets of paper scattered across his desk.

"The smoke of Satan has entered the sanctuary."

He read as he flipped through a book sanctioned by Pope John Paul II several years ago.

"We no longer have to fear the Vatican exposing Satanic pedophilia rites and practices that certain bishops and priests like to amuse themselves with," he read aloud to himself.

He let loose a barrage of laughter.

We no longer have to fear anything. We are in control of our own destiny—no longer bound by the chains of someone else's morality.

Headlines around the world introduced the new pope. The *New York Times* bantered, "American Jew Elected Pope." The article explained, "Joseph Cardinal Steinem of New York City was elected to the papacy after the ninth vote, according to inside information.

"The cardinal electors were solidly divided," the article continued. "An anti-papacy group rallied against those who believed in Petrine authority, with what appeared to be no common ground to share between them in choosing a successor to the assassinated John Paul III.

"Steinem's name came up during the two days of discussion. Slowly, the cardinals favoring Steinem rose to a small majority, then a comfortable majority, and finally to that necessary two-thirds-plus-one majority, taking most cardinal electors by surprise and leaving the diehards on both sides somewhat dazed."

The election was miraculous. Simon Peter laughed to himself, recalling the two cardinals he overheard talking after the vote, "How can people doubt there are signs and miracles in the world today? If anything is miraculous, what happened in the "Upper room" on November 12 is one."

Later, it was revealed that Steinem was the second pope-elect. Cardinal Antonio of Spain had been elected first after several rounds of voting. Then, out of the blue, he removed his name.

Several cardinals, it was rumored, were concerned how, out of nowhere, the American cardinal's name appeared.

It is simply remarkable, Simon Peter thought as he put the newspaper aside, *how easily I drew those cardinals in.*

It was said of the one hundred fifteen men who made up the conclave, some had discarded prayer altogether; some had associated the glory of God with their own ambitions; and some had worked silently for the obliteration of the Petrine office of pope; and Simon Peter knew, most were eager to be bought–favors, money, or position. A few couldn't be bought.

I'll deal with them later, he vowed.

All the lights on her phone lit up at once as if pre-planned. *This is going to be a typical Monday morning.*

Joyce turned from her computer terminal and grabbed the phone. "Mr. Devoe's office. Just a moment, may I ask who's calling? Thank you."

She put the call on hold. *This ought to put him in a good mood.*

"Mr. Devoe, Israel's Prime Minister Itzak Bet is on the line."

Joyce watched a smile spread across his face as he picked up the receiver.

"Prime Minister, how nice to hear from you. What can I do for you, sir?"

"Mr. Devoe, I'll get right to the point. Your offices notified us of the military movement in Syria. As you know, the peace talks regarding the status of Jerusalem are close to completion. But not all parties are happy about it, and I'm concerned about our computer data system. I'm worried that ours may have been compromised. My sources tell me you have the best security program in the world."

Devoe's analytical mind went to work. "When would you like to get together, Prime Minister?" Devoe asked.

"If you'll permit me, Mr. Devoe, I've arranged for you to be picked up tomorrow morning and flown to New York. There my pilot will be waiting to bring you to Israel on a normal diplomatic flight. You'll be the only passenger. It is my utmost concern that our meeting be kept strictly confidential," he stressed.

"I'll be waiting." Devoe hung up the phone and stared out the window at the city below.

I have finally found my way into the power center of the Middle East.

He reached again for the newly released copy of *American Entrepreneur Magazine* containing his story.

It's so nice to be appreciated for who I really am.

He flipped the magazine open to his story and started reading in the middle.

"Devoe easily rallies Americans to himself, regardless of their socio-economic condition. He's a favorite among the disenchanted and those angry with the current administration, the growing national debt, the growing irresponsibility of governmental officials for their actions, and the ever increasing governmental incompetence and waste.

"He views himself as a statesman, a populist who believes in action versus talk."

Devoe closed the magazine and stared at his picture on the cover.

My picture is in every newsstand across the country. Look out, world! Here I come! The working man's savior.

I am the answer to the country's problems.

I'm antigovernment, antiracist, antiauthority, antitrade, anticrime, and antihate. That ought to about cover the whole shooting match.

Even the radical Christians oughta see that I'm the answer to their prayers.

A big grin spread across his face.

They've got to be made to understand that intolerance is the root of all hate in the world.

The last couple of hours had turned the White House into a madhouse, with every reporter in the country either on the phone, in the outer office, or hounding security at the front gate to get in. All of them wanted to know the President's position on the current crisis facing Israel.

Trudy Morris, press secretary and close personal friend of the first family, entered the First Lady's office having just left the White House "War Room." The President was "in conference" and not available at the moment.

"Emily, we've got to get a statement to the press."

"Screw the press. They'll get a statement when I'm good and ready." Emily glared at her.

"Okay, okay, don't get mad at me." Trudy backed up, nearly tripping on her high heels. "I don't care what's going on in Israel," Emily shouted. "They can blow that sore spot off the map as far as I'm concerned. And you know what Bob will say, 'Heck, what's wrong with everybody? Why do you wanna attack Israel? They haven't done anything to deserve this. After all, they gave the Palestinians Jericho. They've signed peace treaties with all their neighbors. What else do you want?' She laughed; a bitter edge hardened her voice.

"His sniveling, whining, cheating voice makes me sick. You'd think, at least while he's in the White House, he'd stay away from those whores and try not to make any more of a public spectacle of me than he already has.

"And get Joni Rains in here. I need some legal advise. Maybe I'll just divorce the jerk. See what that does to his reelection chances–"

"Emily," Trudy interrupted. This wasn't a conversation she cared to be a part of.

"Hurry!" Emily screamed. "Get her now!"

Rabbi Elijah Tzur relaxed as an invisible, gentle circular massage erased the deep frown lines etched on his weathered face. A soft urging began to repeat itself deep in his brain's cavern, "It's time, Elijah. It's time."

He tried to push away the intruding voice and sink deeper into his dreams, but his mind forced itself to the surface of consciousness. He opened his eyes expecting to see the caring face of his wife. Seeing only a soft light from the window and hearing the faint hum of the ceiling fan, he drifted back to sleep.

The gentle massage resumed, and with it the voice. "It's time, Elijah, it's time." He continued to fight consciousness. He reached up to push what he thought were the ministering hands of his wife away, but his arm swished through empty space. Forced awake, he lunged up in the bed. His wife rolled over and continued snoring softly.

Awake after a restless night, he struggled to remember if the conversations he overheard were real or just the dreams of a tired old man.

It's time.... It's time.... What does that mean? Time for what? He reached up, wrinkled hands gently massaging his temple as if to restore his memory. The blaring of a loud siren interrupted his concentration.

What now? Another suicide bomb? Oh, God, how long will this violence go on? How long till You come for Your people?

To some it wasn't a surprise when the world woke up to the banner headlines, "ISRAEL ATTACKED." The controversy over the Temple Mount and the Dome of the Rock doomed any peace agreement before the ink dried.

CNN broadcast day and night the Muslim invasion of Israel. The world was once again treated to front row seats of a war in the Middle East. News commentators expressed shock at the vast and varied coalition of soldiers rushing at the Israeli border.

Six former republics of the Soviet Union and her allies—a coalition of Arab states led by Turkey—had launched an all-out military campaign against Israel. Religious Jews bowed toward the Temple Mount during the attack, praying for deliverance. Around the world, boardroom bets escalated as the hours passed and Israel continued to hang on against impossible odds. Even though the world tried to continue business as usual, ignoring the Middle East was like an alcoholic trying to ignore liquor. Almost everywhere you went, the opportunity existed to catch up on the latest news.

Kaye Howard spent the week listening to radio reports of the attack and wandering to the breakroom, more often than usual, to watch the CNN live coverage of the frantic activity in Jerusalem.

Driving home from the office, she had the radio tuned to KSAT, p.m. News Update of what most reporters were now calling a war.

We're getting close. We need to get out of the city soon, she thought, pulling into the driveway. The calm of the late afternoon was a welcomed relief from the stress at work.

"I'm home." Stale air trapped in the house rushed out the front door. As she put her purse down, twins, Elizabeth and Anne, wrapped themselves around her legs.

"Mommy, mommy," the girls rang out. "Jesus is coming."

Kaye laughed. "Yes, girls, I guess he is. We just don't know when."

She looked at her husband Lee. "Do they know something we don't?"

They laughed at the thought.

"Where's Catherine and Robert?"

"They better be doing their homework. How was work?"

"Awful! The accounting firm that shares the building with us let a bunch of people go this afternoon." She wrinkled up her face.

"I sure picked the wrong time to leave the building. Ugh! I had to ride down the elevator with people carrying boxes, crying, and hugging. It felt like a funeral. The economy is the pits. Maybe we should start thinking about selling the house."

Kaye managed to change clothes as she juggled between putting Elizabeth down and picking Anne up.

"Let's go, girls. Catherine, Robert," Lee yelled as they shuffled through the house to the backyard for their evening walk.

Lee got out the large red wagon while Catherine and Robert got their bikes.

"Come on, Buster," Robert called to the dog as they opened the gate.

Clouds danced in the sky and falling leaves cascaded around the family of six.

They strolled along the row of houses that lined the street and discussed the antics of their four children. Catherine, ten, the oldest, was quickly becoming a young adult.

"So what did you think of Josh's show today?" Kaye kicked a rock and sent it tumbling down the street.

"He's really down on Hollywood," Lee said.

"Well, it's about time people got fed up with the trash they're dishing out. I watched a few minutes of that horrible adult cartoon the other night. They ought to call it 'crude, rude and socially unacceptable.'"

"Hum," he nodded his head.

"I'm getting worried, Lee. The kids are so vulnerable at this age."

"I know," he agreed. "I'm almost afraid to check the different stations when they're in the room. I watched a few minutes of 'Staying in Step' the other night, and the new age overtones were blatantly obvious."

"Garbage, pure garbage, and the young, spongelike minds of kids like ours suck it up before you realize what's going on." Kaye gazed at her four children.

I'm glad they belong to the Lord.

Devoe was in a sour mood. He paced back and forth across his spacious office, frustration building with each step. Suddenly he slammed his fist in the air and cursed. The Muslim coalition had agreed to postpone the movement into Israel until after the next election.

He tried to explain to those hardheaded Russians that once he created his third party he would have more persuasive power over the country regarding American policy toward the conflict.

I won't let them get away with this, he vowed. *I'll fight this till my last breath. They won't know what hit them. This old dog's got teeth, and they may find him attached to the backside of their breeches.*

Devoe clenched his fists. "They'll pay," he screamed. "They'll pay."

In the outer office Joyce heard the commotion.

Oh brother, what now?

After eighteen years of working for the man, she knew he'd never settle down without some distraction. She jumped up, fixed a cup of coffee, and opened the double doors to his office.

Devoe looked up and snarled, "Joyce, don't you know better than to disturb me when I'm busy?"

"Yes, sir, Mr. Devoe. I'm sorry, sir." Joyce smiled to herself. It had been the same routine all these years, but it always brought his blood pressure down and enabled him to focus his energy on something more productive.

"Quit groveling, woman," he hollered. "Give me that coffee and scoot on outta here. You're bothering me."

Joyce quickly closed the heavy oak door behind her.

Devoe sipped the hot coffee. He thought about how well he and Joyce had worked together over the years.

It would be impossible to replace that woman. He grinned and took another sip after savoring the aroma of his favorite flavor, French Vanilla.

After watching the steam rise out of the hot liquid, Devoe's mind went back over his recent trip to Israel. The Israeli government had been most accommodating, and the meeting had gone to Devoe's liking. Prime Minister Itzak Bet had revealed his weak spot. It hadn't taken Devoe long to formulate a plan in his mind, a plan that would entrench him in Israel's deepest secrets.

In conversation, Itzak had explained to Devoe that even though they had agreed in the '93 and '96 peace accords to discuss the status of Jerusalem in the coming years, Israel had no intentions of ever relinquishing control of Jerusalem to the PLO.

Devoe would never forget Itzak's passionate words, "Since we gained control of East Jerusalem, we have done everything possible to open the Old City up to the whole world.

"We have expanded the religious rights of Christians that were severely restricted during the nearly two decades of Jordanian occupation. The Dome of the Rock has remained under the supervision of Muslim authorities, and the city itself has been open to pilgrims even from countries we're still at war with. Israeli sovereignty has not encroached on the religious rights of Muslims, and since the war, the number of Arabs and Jews in Jerusalem has increased.

"With the construction that has taken place by both peoples, it is virtually impossible to separate the two; however, Israel will not relinquish her sovereignty.

"As sure as I'm talking to you now, Jerusalem will remain diverse but undivided. We have confirmed that in the Jerusalem Covenant." Devoe had done his research on the Israeli/PLO agreement, and he had studied the economic growth that had occurred in the Gaza Strip and Jericho after the terrorist factions in the area were controlled.

The main ingredient to building peace in the Middle East rested on an economic foundation from which to build political success, and from all indications Israel and Palestine were well on their way to prosperity.

Free trade zones in the Middle East were flourishing between Israel, Palestine, Jordan, Saudi Arabia, and Egypt. A housing boom that resulted from the area's stability and relaxed zoning by Israel had been the first real spurt of growth.

Devoe knew the only way to force Israel's hand regarding the status of Jerusalem would be to exert global pressure on the Jews with the assistance of non-Palestinian Muslims.

He considered the reason for Israel's interest in his company. Itzak had told him that some members of the Knesset were concerned about the ever-present threat of renewed terrorist plots, especially after the recent assassination of Pope John III.

"Joyce," Devoe summoned by intercom, "I need to send a memo."

"I'll be right there, Mr. Devoe."

Joyce entered the meticulously decorated office with her notepad in hand. She never encouraged her boss to use a tape recorder or dictaphone as many in the building did. She enjoyed the personal interaction.

Devoe propped his boots up on the desk and leaned back in his leather chair. "This is for Mike Jones in Security Engineering.

"Mike, DSI has been hired by the Israeli government to test and secure all access to the central mainframe.

"Our purpose is to prevent terrorists, both from within the nation and from without.

"This has become a critical situation. The ultraorthodox mayor of Jerusalem raveled the delicate fabric that maintained the peace when he promoted talks of rebuilding the Temple.

"In addition, the Israeli government needs some way to process its mounting security data in a place that would be free of any covert action from the Muslims as well as providing a way to track known subversive individuals.

"They have requested that we process their data here in Houston. Our reputation has reached global proportions."

The late afternoon sun played hide-and-seek with the large oak trees that lined the street. Kaye waved at the neighbors and admired their neatly groomed lawn.

"Did you catch the news?" she asked Lee. "Have they reported anymore about the flooding in Missouri?"

"Mom," Catherine interrupted, "can Robert and I ride our bikes to the corner?"

"Yes, but watch for cars backing out of their driveways. And don't go past the corner till Dad and I catch up."

Kaye and Lee laughed as Buster, the family's small black-and-white Boston Terrier, ran after the kids. His tongue flew up to his ear, sending slobber trailing behind him.

Kaye glanced over and admired Lee's dark hair and the few white strands around his temple.

"No," Lee said, returning to their conversation. "I missed it. I didn't get home till right before you did."

"I guess Gloria fed the kids?" she asked.

"Yeah, they were just finishing up when I got home."

"You hungry?" Kaye asked.

"No, I had a big lunch."

The conversation lagged as they watched the kids race to the corner.

"Flooding on one side of the globe and raging fires destroying half of California," Kaye said more in thought than in conversation.

"So what?" Lee asked, lost in his own thoughts.

"Oh, I was just thinking about the fires in California and the flooding in the Midwest," she said.

Lee reflected on the recent disasters. "It's as if God is bringing people to their knees, anything to remove the worldliness and cause us to open our eyes and seek His face."

"I heard on the Josh Cohen Show yesterday that the fire could have been avoided. A man from Malibu called in and explained how the National Forest Service in California wanted to start a controlled burn in early spring to get rid of all the overgrowth before the circular winds of fall hit. Some environmentalist whackos objected and blocked it because of an "endangered" bird nesting there." "What idiots. I hope they're happy now." Lee shook his head in exasperation.

"Quote, endangered birds–" Kaye motioned in the air with two fingers– "burned out and six counties declared a National Disaster. "And get this," she added, "someone else called the show and told Josh about an Arizona newspaper editor who had written an editorial suggesting that the wind and fire had a conference and conspired to burn down the homes of the rich."

"That's unbelievable," Lee whistled.

"And," she went on, "the editor called it poetic justice that a homeless person, shivering in the '70 degree' cold, built a fire to keep warm and had made the rich homeless.

"Just you wait, liberals are going to use this fire in California as a platform for vagrants." Lee looked back to check on the girls.

"You couldn't pay me enough to live in California," Kaye said.

"Yeah, they've got it all, riots, fires, earthquakes, and mud slides." Lee shrugged.

I wonder what's next? Kaye grew reflective.

Buster pranced back to the wagon, dodging the four little hands reaching out to grab him.

The clouds shuffled for position, the air got heavy, and the sky grew dark. A stiff breeze blew through the trees that lined the street, jostling long twisted branches back and forth. Kaye and Lee hurried the kids toward home.

Two cats raced across the street and a flock of birds shot out of the trees above….the wind picked up and swirled debris around Buster. He began running in circles. Lightening flashed across the sky.

Buster searched the empty wagon. He ran back and forth between discarded bicycles searching for the children who had ridden them only moments before. He stuck his small snout in the air and began howling a lonely sound that lasted well into the night.

The enemy outnumbered Israeli military five to one. Israeli's Deputy of Defense General Leiberman, a crusty old man of the old guard who had long since lost his will to fight, placed a desperate call to the prime minister.

"Itzak, we've got to have some help. We're outnumbered five to one. You've got to call the White House. Call the United Nations. Call somebody, man! We've kept the ground troops at the borders, but our cities will be invaded by nightfall. We are literally at the verge of being driven into the sea. Obliterated forever!"

The receiver toppled into its cradle. Itzak stared at the wall, recounting his earlier conversation with Secretary of State Wilson Johnson. It was painfully obvious that Israel would not survive the awesome numbers assembled against her, and Campbell had confirmed his worst fears. The United States would not take any action without the approval of the UN Security Council.

Itzak slumped in his chair. Bleak despair descended over him. He rubbed his face in his hands. Would he be the first to fire? The one to start what the world feared most? Would his name be cursed by generations to come? Was it his destiny to start a nuclear war?

Itzak felt the first signs of panic rising in his stomach. "What do I do? This can't be the end. Give me a sign!" he demanded of the heavens.

Is this a test, like the Six Day War? But we won that one. Surely God won't take this land from us again?

He searched the recesses of his mind for the Words of God, but he couldn't find any. He hadn't opened the Torah for sixty-five years. The knot in his stomach tightened.

In the midst of sirens screaming through the city, bombs exploding throughout the countryside, and blasts of guns announcing the approaching masses of ground troops with the intent of the utter destruction of Israel, a miracle occurred. The heavens opened and the earth erupted. Russian bombers, fighters, and attack aircraft hurtled to the ground. Tanks and ground troops toppled over as the ground lurched and split, opening up to swallow Israel's enemy.

The seas roared, waves pitched and tossed, vomiting out submarines and Russian aircraft carriers. Volcanoes in the Golan Heights, dormant for centuries, spewed forth fiery sulfur that rained down on unsuspecting enemy forces. Ashes blasting into the atmosphere caused clouds overhead to burst open and empty torrential rains, and large hailstones poured down on the doomed.

Confusion ruled. Allied Muslim forces filled with hate for the Jews began warring against each other. Within hours, the enemy gathered against Israel was destroyed. Devastation and human carnage littered the ground. The world watched with timidity as the deadliest battle in history came to an abrupt end. Israel timidly peeked her head out to observe the devastation at the Almighty's hand. Hearts swelled for the love of God. Secular Jews once again praised the God of Abraham, Isaac, and Jacob.

2

"It had a great and high wall, with twelve gates, and at the gates twelve angels; and names were written on them, which are those of the twelve tribes of the sons of Israel.
And the material of the wall was jasper; and the city was pure gold, like clear glass. The foundation stones of the city wall were adorned with every kind of precious stone.
The first foundation stone was jasper; the second, sapphire; the third, chalcedony; the fourth, emerald; the fifth, sardonyz; the sixth, sardius; the seventh, chrysolite; the eighth, beryl; the ninth, topaz; the tenth, chrysoprase; the eleventh, jacinth; the twelfth, amethyst.
And the twelve gates were twelve pearls; each one of the gates was a single pearl.
And the street of the city was pure gold, like transparent glass."
(Revelation 21:12, 18-21) (NAS)

Heaven appeared and the throne of God shone, a sea of glass, like crystal, separated the saints from the Lord. The flashing of lightning, voices, and peals of thunder were heard.

Four living creatures worshiped before Him, crying out, "Holy, Holy, Holy is the Lord God, the Almighty, who was and who is and who is to come."

They were all there, the raptured saints, the living and the dead. The multitudes fell down before Him and one by one approached...and their works were tested. The wood and stubble were consumed in a fiery blaze, the heat of which caressed their faces and burned in their hearts.

Kaye stood up, and tears streamed down her face as she looked at the scant offering lying at His feet. He reached out and gently wiped her eyes. She was home at last, embraced in the arms of the Father. The tears were dried, the guilt and the sorrow erased. Joy pulsed through Kaye's body.

Voices of praise, from millions and millions of angels mingled with the voices of the saints, cried out "Glory be to God."

Millions, robed in white shining garments, were laughing and shouting, "Hallelujah! Salvation and glory and power belong to our Lord and God."

Kaye marveled at the streets of pure gold, like clear glass. She didn't know how long she'd been praising and worshiping at the Throne.

A large angel appeared, issuing invitations to the great supper. Kaye had an uncontrollable urge to sing and shout again, coupled with a burning desire to know the Father's plan for the earth.

Angels going about their duties outnumbered the saints. She approached one. "What's happening on the earth?"

"You'll have to ask the archangel Michael."

"Where is he?" Her eagerness reflected back in her eyes as it bounced of the radiant being before her.

"He's battling with Satan in New York. The very airwaves"– the angel rolled his eyes– "are vibrating with cunning lies and disgusting filth, and it's all being transmitted from New York City.

"Satan, in the disguise of morality and tradition, from one side of his mouth, takes the truth and corrupts it by leaving out the reason for the Truth's existence and then," the angel lamented, "from the other side of his foul mouth he utters profanity, reveres harlots, and advocates pornography."

Abhorrence showed on the angel's glowing face. "We've had many battles in New York City, the global center of social, political, cultural, and commercial life," he explained. "It's the city where the bodies and souls of men and women are bought and sold, the city where the best dressed of all the world parade their designer fashions and costly garments. New York is the city of a million Jews."

This large beautiful angel in front of her stomped his foot. Kaye marveled at God's messenger. A flutter of his wing brought her attention back to the conversation. "Now that the church has been removed, Satan's legion of demons have free reign and evil is rampant. The archangel Michael is battling for God's truth," he said.

"Satan is employing a seldom-used tactic, disguising himself as goodness, which is subjective instead of absolute. He is talking values, prayer in schools, religion, traditional family structure and a return to the political right. I have to admit it's a theme that sells.

"Of course," he paused and snickered, "now that those of the great I Am have been removed, his audience is not quite as large as it was." The angel's voice rang with energy and boldness. "The Jews," he continued, "have realized there is a spiritual problem in the world, and the rapture caused many to evaluate their lives and their relationship to God." He shook his head.

"Millions are flocking to anyone claiming to know the answers, anyone and anything but the Savior.

"Now is the time for God's chosen people. Michael is busy with the details." Kaye searched the angel's vivid eyes as he spoke the words of God.

"It says in 1 John 4:1 not to believe every spirit, but to test the spirits to see whether they are from Him, because many false prophets have gone out into the world. And that," the angel assured her, "is blatantly evident on the earth right now."

Kaye recalled the titles of books on the bestsellers list before the rapture. Self help, new age, and numerous other similar type books were selling by the millions. Gurus traveled around the world conducting seminars on how to cure yourself by calling forth the positive power from within.

"Will Michael return soon?" she asked. "I'd like to know what events led up to the exposure of the Antichrist. What happened after the rapture? Did any natural disasters occur as a result? How are the lost ten tribes of Israel revealed. What will be the events that occur as a result of God's judgments? And most importantly will my Jewish friends ever see the Kingdom of God?" Kaye ran out of breath.

The angel chuckled. "We were told there would be those of you seeking to know time and events. Have patience," he said. "Michael will return soon."

The papal inauguration of Pope Simon Peter II was attended by presidents, kings, dictators, terrorists, and rabbis. Surprisingly, even amid global chaos, most world leaders felt it important enough to attend the inauguration. The upper room was filled to capacity with the two hundred eighty dignitaries present.

The pope, televised to the four corners the globe and simultaneously into fourteen languages, gave his blessing and welcomed all the peoples and the religions of the world into the arms of the Church Universal.

"The love of God is for all peoples and nations. All religions are equal in God's eyes," he assured the world.

Once Simon Peter finished his performance for the world, he summoned an unknown rabbi he'd met in Israel the previous year.

Monsignor Paul Lucci, the pope's personal secretary, showed Rabbi Deri in.

Simon extended his hand for the traditional show of reverence to his authority.

"You'll excuse me," Rabbi Deri said, ignoring the pope's gesture as he made his way to a chair.

Simon glared but chose to ignore the affront.

"So…" Rabbi Deri broke the awkward silence. "To what do I owe this private audience with your eminence?"

Simon put his hands together, cradled his chin with this two thumbs, touched his lips with his forefingers, and studied the Rabbi for a moment.

"I wanted to thank you in person on behalf of John Paul II for your assistance last year. John Paul came close to destroying all the groundwork the inner circle had accomplished over the years to the keep the masses in tow.

"He had become too rigid, too fundamental, too exclusive—too devout. He had to be eliminated."

Simon smiled at the rabbi. "I'm sure you understand. After John Paul III issued his encyclical letter 'Love Is Perfected in Obedience,' the church was called intolerant. People are more advanced than that now. Obedience is outdated. We must allow people to be guided by the truth from within. Don't you agree, Rabbi?"

"You may be right. But what exactly are you trying to say?" Rabbi Deri snapped.

Simon was growing increasingly irritated at the rabbi. *This is not how the inner circle promised this meeting would go.*

Simon decided to get right to the point. "I have received word from God through a vision of the blessed mother." He collected his thoughts and continued. "She appeared to me and revealed that the world is in danger. There is a population explosion. The earth can no longer sustain billions of people. We have destroyed our resources and polluted our rivers and skies. Greed and division have fostered worldwide destruction. The three largest religions must now come together for the sake of the good earth.

"She told me that when we've accomplished this unity, then the Messiah would return to earth and rule."

Rabbi Deri finally smiled. "This is all you wanted to tell me? I already know the arrival of Messiah is imminent."

He stood up, ending the meeting. "You're welcome for the help we provided last year, but I would submit to you that you have much more of a problem ahead of you than before."

Rabbi Deri turned and left the room, leaving Simon speechless.

How dare he! I'm not like all those other popes who were afraid of Israel. I'll show them what power really is. I'm just the pope to give birth to the new Church.

"Your Holiness." Monsignor Lucci burst into the room. "Is there a problem? Rabbi Deri looked kind of strange when he left just now."

Simon burst into a fit of laughter. "Strange, you say. Yes, he is a little strange."

Simon felt an unexpected liking for this young secretary of his. "So, tell me, monsignor, what brought someone of your youth to this position?"

The young priest blushed. "You haven't heard, sir?"

"No, I haven't heard. And, for future reference, I don't like playing games."

"Sorry, sir. I've just heard rumors that I was a close relative of my last boss, His Holiness."

"Oh!" Simon sat down. New interest in his secretary surfaced.

"Have a seat, son." He motioned toward the chair Rabbi Deri had just vacated.

"So tell me a little about our previous Holiness. Being from America I didn't have an opportunity to spend much time with him."

"Well, he seemed to have a lot of enemies. A vocal group of cardinals, bishops, prominent theologians, and laypeople had joined forces to oppose Pope John Paul III and the papacy. A group who, for various reasons, discarded their Catholic faith, choosing instead to embrace the things of this world."

Paul stopped talking and looked up from his hands to if see if the pope was still listening.

"I'm sure you've been briefed, Holiness, on the problems the church suffers from, not just including doctrinal questions and papal authority, but liberation theology has spread rapidly through the third-world countries with the clergy openly promoting Marxist Christianity.

"Why, Holiness, it has even become popular to be known in some circles as a nonbelieving cleric, lesbian nun, or homosexual priest, bishop, or cardinal. This truly grieved Pope John Paul. In two thousand years of the Roman Catholic Church's existence, there has never been anything like the church today."

Paul saw an odd smile on the pope's face and a faraway look in his eyes.

"My son, it's a different world we live in. My job is to let the faithful believe what they want to believe and let them live how they want to live. I've got to tickle their ears. But no matter what else, they've got to believe they can't enjoy the fruits of heaven on earth without this pope."

Simon Peter knew the power was in believing that the pope holds the keys to the gates of heaven and hell. He roared a deep laugh, seeing the innocent look on his secretary's face.

"You can get back to your work now, son." Simon waved his hand toward the door in dismissal.

As Paul left, Simon pushed away from his ornate mahogany desk and tread barefoot across his ancient Persian rug to the couch.

He skooched down, nestling into the cool leather of his couch, and contemplated his good fortune and craftiness.

His mind drifted back to the murder of John Paul III in Israel.

A close relative, hum....

Simon tried to picture a resemblance between the boy and John Paul.

I wonder if the little episode that brought forth young Paul inspired his strong virtuous rhetoric that nearly destroyed our plans? Killing him before he blocked my takeover plans was easier than we expected, Simon thought. *Surely he suspected after that bout of the "flu." Either that or he was stupider than I thought.* Simon snickered at the thought. *Too bad he wouldn't cooperate and just die in bed like Pope John Paul I.*

Blaming that car explosion on the Intifada was a stroke of genius. Even if it was Rabbi Deri's idea. Things couldn't have worked out better than if it had all been "divine" providence.

They appeared out of nowhere. No one knew their names or any of their relatives. A rumor started that they came from the United States and were living in Hebron with an ultra-orthodox sect of Jews. But no one could find anyone who had ever had contact with them.

They were obviously Jews but didn't look or dress like the orthodox, other than dressing in all black, so who could really know for sure?

The word spread quickly of their arrival and of the message they proclaimed. It didn't take long for the rabbis–traditional, orthodox, and liberal–to unite in their effort to remove these two from the Wailing Wall. After all, how could any self-respecting Jew come for daily prayers only to be assaulted by these two who were constantly talking about the Messiah as if he'd already come and gone!

People pressed forward to get a glimpse of the two vagrants shouting their blasphemy at the crowd. "Repent! The Kingdom of God is at hand."

"Kooks! Extremists!" yelled someone.

"Hatemongers! Fanatics!" yelled another.

The area grew thick with bodies pressed against one another hoping to catch a glimpse of the men who dared cause such a ruckus.

"Children of Israel, the time is at hand. Your Messiah has come. You must turn from your wicked ways and seek His face."

The anger exploding from the crowd became violent. Fruit bombarded the two men and splattered against the Wall—the colorful stains creating a collage on a dull background.

"Judgment is coming upon the earth. Your crops will perish from lack of rain. Your animals will die. The earth will shake, and your buildings will tumble to the ground. Repent and seek the Lord!"

The crowd exploded. Weapons of fruit were soon exchanged for rocks. Hateful words and curses drowned out the words of the prophets of doom.

Foreign journalists rushed to the Old City, each hoping to get the story on the wire first.

"There's gonna be blood, Irene," a cameraman said as he slammed the door behind them. "I told you we didn't want to leave Jerusalem too soon. Mark my words, this is the place to be."

"Yeah, well, won't Tom Donnelly, America's beloved anchorman, be excited? He just loves a good fight."

3

"Behold, I stand at the door and knock;
if anyone hear my voice and open the door,
I will come in to him and will dine
with him, and he with Me.
He who overcomes, I will grant to him to sit
down with Me on My throne, as I also overcame
and sat down with My Father on His throne.
He who has an ear, let him hear
what the Spirit says to the churches."
(Rev. 3:20-22) (NAS)

Harry parked the car and ran to his apartment. The Cowboys/Dolphin Monday night football game was about to start. He had little interest in TV, other than the Dallas Cowboys and select documentaries.

I've got to stop working late, he told himself.

His stomach growled.

Forget the pregame introduction, I'm hungry.

He grabbed the remote control on his way to the kitchen and hit the power button. As he passed the couch he felt strange—dizzy. He plopped down on the sofa.

The TV flickered on and the football commentators skidded back and forth in their chairs. After a few minutes of watching the set shake, the screen suddenly went black.

Harry froze. He stared at the black screen for several minutes. "What the..." The audio sounded with an alert signal.

"We interrupt this program...the national earthquake center in Golden, Colorado, reports an undetermined number of simultaneously occurring earthquakes. The center has registered earthquakes in California as ranging between 8.4 to 8.9 on the Richter scale. Quakes in other parts of the world are estimated between 7.5 and 8.6. Pandemonium and confusion are reported around the world."

The news announcer paused as sounds of shuffled paper replaced his voice. "We are now receiving information from the BCN (British Cable Network) and RFT (Russian Free Television). Police stations and missing person bureaus are being overwhelmed by frantic calls from people claiming a mysterious vanishing of family members. In addition to reports of property damage and injuries, strange reports of disappearances and UFO sightings here in the United States are flooding in."

Panic crept into the announcer's voice. More sounds of rustled papers added to the suspense of listeners.

"Police officials... are... answering as many distress calls as is possible, however... they request that only those reporting life-threatening situations call 911... in order to alleviate overloaded phone lines."

The visual signal flashed back on. Harry just stared at the TV.

Drops of sweat appeared on the announcer's brow as minutes stretched into an hour.

"At this time missing person reports are not being treated as emergency calls.... Excuse me," the young man apologized, interrupted by a stack of reports pushed in front of him. "Due to the enormous volume of information coming over the news wire, the system is operating intermittently." He wiped his brow with a handkerchief. "According to initial reports, it is confirmed that simultaneous earthquakes have occurred worldwide."

The announcer paused and adjusted his glasses. "We are receiving similar reports from Canada, Mexico, Brazil, Africa, India, China, Japan, Australia, Israel, Spain, and Germany."

The newsman waved away the camera, emotionally unable to continue.

The network switched to its Washington affiliate standing by for a White House announcement. Viewers around the world tuned into the FOX Network experienced rising alarm. International phone lines were overloaded, and the atmosphere vibrated with the hopeless wails of billions.

Harry stumbled into the bedroom of his modest two bedroom apartment and opened the drawer of his bedside table, searching for his address book. His eyes rested on the rarely noticed monogrammed Bible he had been given last Hanukkah, of all times.

Why do I insist on keeping that?

He placed an unsteady hand on the phone. His hand began to shake as he visualized his friend Kaye. He remembered how her eyes glistened, the never-ending stories about girlhood friends, antics at college, her daily challenges, goals and dreams. He suddenly thought of their conversations, the narrow span of the luncheon table that separated them. He remembered her passionate explanation of some biblical passage and its significance to "end times."

Harry chuckled, thinking how she was forever popping her head in his office to tell him about a good Christian novel or prophecy book she'd just read, or explaining something new she'd learned in her Bible study class.

He marveled at her natural joy, the light in her eyes, the dance in her step...her assurance of a "rapture"...her firm convictions of Jesus and His second coming.

Harry hesitantly picked up the phone and dialed Kaye's number. Surprisingly, even in the midst of what the media portrayed as worldwide death and destruction caused by the earthquakes and the mass confusion and casualties of the unexplained vaporization of millions, the call went through.

One ring, two rings, Harry's fears began to explode in his mind. Three rings.

Someone would have picked up the phone by now.

Four rings.

"Hello, this is Lee. Kaye and I are unable to come to the phone. At the sound of the tone, please leave a message and we'll return your call as soon as possible."

The beep blared yet was stifled by the void in Harry's mind, making it sound light years away as he slowly put the receiver down.

A terrifying fear squeezed his heart. *Please, God, let this be a dream.* Yet he knew leaving a message would be useless. His call would never be returned. He fell to his knees. Shame consumed him, his sins besieged him—sins he had never recognized nor admitted even existed in his life. Suddenly emptied, he felt he was in a vacuum—all the philosophical and scientific beliefs that had made up his essence, torn into small pieces and pitched in the wind. The useless baggage and excuses he'd amassed over the years in an effort to deny Jesus as the Messiah crashed down around him.

His head pounded. Blood pulsed to its limits. His eyes blurred. His ears rang. In his emptiness and despair he cried out, "Dear God, why was I so blind? Why didn't I listen?"

"Help me." Tears streaked down his face. "Forgive me..."

The horns in heaven rang out and the angels rejoiced. Once again, another lost sheep from the House of Israel had been found.

A loud voice rang from the heavens.

"I will make their boys their officials; mere children will govern them...Jerusalem staggers, Judah is falling; their words and deeds are against the Lord, defying his glorious presence...Youths oppress my people, women rule over them. O my people, your guides lead you astray; they turn you from the path...What do you mean by crushing my people and grinding the faces of the poor? declares the Lord, the Lord almighty" (Isaiah 3:4, 8, 12, 15).

The rest of America watched as Emily Wells, First Lady, approached the podium in the State Department briefing room. Behind her were cabinet members located in the crisis. Joni Rains,

Attorney General, Deanne Shannon, Secretary of Health and Human Services, Mary Burns, United Nations Ambassador and Libby Goldberg, Supreme Court Justice. Also gathered around the dais were other women cabinet members and close personal friends of the First Lady.

The picture captured on TV struck an odd cord in millions of Americans. The First Lady looked calm, dressed in a black turtleneck and deep burgundy suit. A gold necklace and a simple gold bracelet adorned her ensemble, plain pearl studs pierced her ears. The official seal hung on the wall behind her.

"Ladies and gentlemen of the press and beloved Americans, I come to you in a time of dire crisis." She scanned the room. "The President and the Vice President have become victims of what has been determined by the attorney general's office, to be a right wing, terrorist action." Reporters madly scribbled to get every word, not pausing to consider their own reaction.

"While watching a football game in our private quarters this evening, the President was kidnapped and the Vice President was shot in the struggle." Emily stopped, unable to be heard over the gasps emanating from the press corps.

"We haven't received instructions from the terrorists, but we'll brief you as details permit." She glanced at her notes. "The Speaker of the House cannot be found, and the American people can no longer trust the members of Congress or the Senate." Emily paused to wipe a tear.

"Ladies and gentlemen, we are in the midst of an international crisis. Enemies from within have stolen our leader, and mother nature has inflicted her displeasure on us. In response, I'm declaring a state of emergency. I have activated the Federal Emergency Management Act (FEMA), Executive Order 12148 and marshal law until this crisis has passed."

A pan around the room revealed the affirmative nods of reporters, giving Emily the assurance she needed of media endorsement.

"I know I have your support as I appropriate presidential authority. I have contacted world leaders and assured them that the United States government is in control and fully capable of assisting in all global and humanitarian aid, supporting her allies and fulfilling our UN responsibilities. I also want to assure the world that everything possible is being done to return the President to the loving arms of his family and country."

Emily concluded her briefing with a barely visible smile touching her lips.

Emily Wells, now acting President of the United States turned and left the room, escaping further questions. White House Press Secretary Trudy Morris continued the briefing.

Bradley Dunn, a reporter with NBC, raised his hand.

"Trudy, these are serious accusations that some right-wing group has kidnapped the President and murdered the Vice President. What proof does the attorney general's office have? And has the White House received any response from congressional members or senators regarding Emily's implementation of Executive Order 12148, and her usurpation of the presidency? And what investigations, if any, are being conducted into the sudden UFO sightings, and the massive disappearances, or vaporizations as some have suggested?"

The accusation in his voice didn't go unnoticed.

"Brad, I agree that these are serious times and we can't jump to conclusions. But after previous terrorist attacks in this country, the attorney general's office has sufficient proof to suggest a right-wing conspiracy. And, as you know, both the House and the Senate are in recess. And at this point neither the massive disappearances nor the UFOs have been officially confirmed. However," she continued, "the White House has been notified of a rash of suicides. It appears, some individuals were unable to accept the serious repercussions of their acts of treason."

Trudy charged on, her voice growing louder. "This terrorist action of right-wing conspiracy groups will go down in history, exposing their true characteristics, as not even the Watergate scandal could do."

Trudy turned her attention to another. "Yes, Alice."

Brad refused to be dismissed. "Trudy, this has all happened so fast. How has the FBI been able to determine a Christian Right takeover verses the very real possibility of a UFO abduction?"

"Don't be absurd," Trudy gasped. "I refuse to consider such ridiculous suggestions."

Alice Freidman, CBS correspondent, stood up. "Trudy, does the White House expect to hear from the Supreme Court regarding Emily's assuming the top governmental position?"

Trudy moved aside, still visibly angry. "I'll let Justice Goldberg give you the position of the court."

Goldberg stepped to the podium and adjusted the microphone. "I have spoken to several of the justices who have given their full support to the First Lady. In the absences of the Vice President and Speaker of the House, they are in full agreement that Emily is the most logical person to work with the attorney general's office in getting to the bottom of this terrorist action."

Alice stood up again. "What about the justices you haven't talked to?"

Goldberg bristled. "As to the other justices" –she cleared her throat– "they've been unavailable. However, I'm sure they will also fully support the First Lady."

A man, unfamiliar to many in the room stood up and said, "Ms. Morris, I'm Todd Adams, editor of the World Council of Churches Daily News. Usually one of my reporters would cover this briefing. However, they appear to be casualties of one disaster or another.

"My questions are, first, what is the White House's response to the alarmists' cry that the world is coming to an end? And second, are the millions of disappearances due to an ascension to a higher spiritual plane for advanced souls?"

Trudy uncharacteristically paused to word her next statement carefully. "Mr. Adams, the First Lady, uh, President pro tem, will be working around the clock with her advisors and will address the nation tomorrow with specifics of how the White House intends to assist those devastated by earthquakes and how we'll work hand-in-hand with the UN.

"And, Mr. Adams" – she looked him in the eye – "I assure you the White House does not believe the world is coming to an end. As far as some ascension to a higher spiritual plane, well, Mr. Adams, you, the editor of a religious and highly acclaimed publication, are obviously here. If anything, the people missing have been removed because they hindered the spiritual freedom of others. Frankly, Mr. Adams, I don't think you can attribute to the gods this disaster inflicted on us by Mother Nature and the Christian Right."

Being a conservative, middle-aged white man did not make Harry a politically correct person. He had not voted for Bob Wells, and he was opposed to the participation his wife, Emily, had had in cabinet appointments and public policy-making.

The press secretary's voice grated on his nerves as he watched rerun after rerun of the White House briefing from the safety of his own bedroom. He studied the expressions of each woman gathered around the podium—women hand-picked by Emily to hold powerful cabinet positions, women wrapped in a web of international secrecy, women who were members of either the Council on Foreign Relations, the Trilateral Commission, or the Bilderbergers—organizations whose goals included bringing an end to American dominance, and installing a global, One World Order of which they would be on the ground floor of power.

It had been reported after their respective Senate confirmations that these cabinet women were a diverse collection of militant lesbians, feminist new-agers, anti-Christian activists, sex perverts, doctrinal Marxists, and global elitists. Just observing that group of women together on TV was enough to make any decent, law-abiding citizen experience a cramping dread in the pit of the stomach.

Harry channel surfed, stopping at CNN and various other news reports of the global earthquakes. Raging fires blazed around the globe, and power outages made it impossible for people to communicate with loved ones.

As night descended like an ominous shroud on half the world, all rescue efforts stopped. Billions of people huddled, cloaked in darkness—lying awake in a hopeless state of panic, which chased away any hope of peace that a moment's sleep might have provided. Most occupants of the world, smothered in despair, spent another long, petrifying night without power, water, or communication.

4

"For false Christs and
false prophets will rise
and show signs and
wonders to deceive, if
possible, even the elect."
(Mark 13:22) (NKJV)

Kaye waited for Michael, the archangel, to return from another battle. As she prayed for her Jewish friends on earth, she recalled that August Monday morning when she turned the radio on her desk to the Democracy In Action Network and her favorite talk radio program. "It's 11:06. Stay tuned for the Josh Cohen Show," the announcer said.

She remembered her enthusiasm at having Josh back after his being gone for a week. Representative Tom Davis, who filled in for Josh, had done a good job keeping the listeners abreast of current events while Josh was on his "secret mission," but no one stimulated her mind and echoed her thoughts like Josh Cohen. She typed the name and address on a form letter she was getting ready to mail as the program began. The beat of the music that she knew by heart bounced off the four walls of her office and the program began.

"Now from our studio in New York City, welcome to the DIA Network. You are listening to a special edition of the Josh Cohen Show."

Josh's opening monologue began. His excitement was obvious and his voice commanded the attention of his audience. "Greetings, friends and fellow chatters. I know you have been anxious to learn of my whereabouts this past week, so I'll keep you in suspense no longer. I'm going to tell you about the most educational and enlightening week I spent in Israel."

Kaye's dad walked into her office with a fresh cup of coffee. Listening to Josh was a daily routine. "What's he talking about today?"

"Josh was in Israel last week," she hurried to explain, not wanting to miss anything.

Josh embarked into his long detailed account of how he'd come to visit Israel.

"I've always had a standing invitation from friends to visit Israel. While traveling one weekend with my favorite sports team during the playoffs, I got to know Dave Malone, the coach fairly well. In a conversation, Dave had casually mentioned that he and his family had a strong desire to visit Israel someday.

"Dave's family are Christians, but they're not the kind of people who wear it on their sleeves, so you wouldn't necessarily know it unless you know them well. Since Dave and his family were going to be in Europe in the next couple of months for a sports event, I suggested that we get together and meet in Israel for a vacation.

"We made plans and reservations were booked and confirmed, but while in Europe, Dave's son became seriously ill and required emergency surgery. Dave's family had to fly back to the States, and because of the illness, they were unable to meet me in Israel.

"Needless to say, I was very disappointed about having to cancel the trip. After thinking about it, and realizing that arrangements for a guest host had been made and that everything was in place, I decided to proceed with my trip to Israel."

Kaye worked at her desk while listening, suffering aggravating interruptions throughout the show.

After laying out the background for the reason of his trip and its near cancellation, Josh continued with his monologue, not stopping to take a commercial break, eager to share his excitement of his trip.

"If any of you out there across the bountiful plain have never been to Israel, I would encourage you to put it on the list of places you'd like to visit. Really!" he exclaimed to his staff.

Josh regularly responded to the facial expressions of his production staff in the sound booth as they screened callers and joked with him. "I realize Israel is not a place an average individual would normally think of going on a vacation, not even if you're Jewish," he continued, "but the rich history of that ancient land is something you don't want to miss."

He grew introspective. "The holocaust museum made a lasting impression on my psyche. I can't believe there are people who have the gall to claim it never happened."

"The country is beautiful–lush green hills and beautiful flowers dot the landscape," he reflected. "Of course I enjoyed seeing holy sites, but I didn't just spend time as a tourist." Josh paused for a moment to lightly tap, tap, tap on his desk, building the suspense.

"I had the pleasure of a private briefing and discussion with Prime Minister Itzak Bet about the Israeli 'peace talks.'"

Kaye's mouth flew open. "What! How did he arrange a meeting with the prime minister of Israel?" she asked her father. "He's not a head of state. He's not even part of the government. And of all places, why Israel? Why was he so important that Israel would take time to brief him on the peace talks?"

Kaye had to stop from going ballistic and focus back on the radio show.

Josh continued, "I also enjoyed a briefing with the foreign affairs Minister and the minister of defense. We discussed how Israel, a tiny country surrounded by a hostile people, could so successfully defend herself from her enemies."

All that week Josh slipped in some additional tidbit about his trip to Israel. He gave details of the political arena in Israel and explained the various personality conflicts between the prime minister and the Minister of Foreign Affairs Benjamin Sadle.

Apparently Josh had established a fairly good rapport with Sadle, because later in the week he casually mentioned a phone conversation they'd had while Sadle had been in Washington for a meeting with Secretary of State Johnson.

Kaye remembered a particular caller that week who asked Josh why he thought Sadle was seeking his council and Josh responded, "Israel is looking for the truth, and they want the light of truth to shine down on them."

Josh was a real cut-up on the air. He had a way of saying things sarcastically. Oftentimes it was hard to tell if Josh believed the statement himself or if he was simply making fun of the caller.

After listening to the show for the last three-plus years, Kaye had seen a pattern of egotism develop and had come to the conclusion that Josh really thought he was the "truth" and the "light."

As Josh elaborated on his talks with Sadle, his fierce opposition to the peace talks surprised her.

"They've got them right where they want them," he shouted, referring to Israel. "The Berlin Wall is down, Russia is embroiled in a political and economic collapse, and there are no large communist countries left to give money and support to the PLO terrorists except China—and they don't do nothin' for nobody."

He continued ranting. "The United States is not overly fond itself of Abduel Hussein, the PLO leader, especially after he sided with King Sherif when Iraq invaded Kuwait.

"Israel," he said proudly as if it were his homeland, "has proven her ability to whip any Arab nation foolish enough to attack.

"All you have to do," he explained, "is look at the Israeli victories in the Six Day War, the Yom Kipper War, and their superb ability to control the ongoing Intifada. Land negotiations do not have to be part of these talks.

"Abduel Hussein does not hold any negotiating chips. He's powerless without Soviet sponsorship."

Josh was incredulous at Israel's belief that it had to negotiate with the PLO because the U.S. insisted on it. He had been shocked at Sadle's acknowledgment that Israel felt it imperative to have the backing of the United States, even though the treaty had been negotiated in secret in Norway without the participation of the U.S. Josh made an effort not to be negative, but his subtle innuendoes caused many listeners to realize that he didn't believe the agreement would last.

It was still dark Tuesday morning at 4:30 when Devoe jumped out of bed. It was a habit he'd acquired in the service. He dressed, went downstairs, and poured a steaming cup of coffee from the pot programmed to come on the same time every day.

Occasionally his wife would join him for coffee and a danish, but not today. He wasn't surprised she hadn't heard him. He had insisted years ago that they maintain separate bedrooms. He snored and she liked to read late at night. Each kept the other awake. Separate rooms had been the easiest solution.

He thought about taking her a cup of coffee. It was rare that he stayed gone for a three-day weekend, but he hadn't been hunting in a long time and decided he deserved a break. He had gotten home too late Monday night to wake her. But he was in a hurry.

I'll call her later in the day, he thought, rushing out to the car.

He noticed there wasn't the usual traffic on the freeways. He passed the sites of several traffic accidents. Curious, he turned on the radio for the news.

"Latest reports on the earthquakes indicate the most severe damage occurred in San Francisco, Tokyo, Moscow, Istanbul, and the Middle East. The death toll is staggering and is climbing as rescue efforts continue. At this time, worldwide counts of the dead or missing are reaching into the billions."

"What on earth," Devoe murmured.

"All U.S. nuclear reactors have been shut down for observation, and residents in vicinities of reactors are urged to remain indoors," the news report continued.

Devoe tightened his grip on the steering wheel. It was as if he'd been in a different world the last several days. While he'd enjoyed the rare opportunity for total isolation, the world had come crashing down.

He sped up, anxious to get to the office and see what damage, if any, had been done to his empire. 8:00 a.m. rolled around and Devoe glanced at his watch. *Where on earth could Joyce be? She's usually here by* 7:45. He got up from his desk, experiencing an uneasiness.

As he walked through the building he noticed empty desks and a lack of the usual activity that characterized the start of a week. His thoughts went immediately to a takeover attempt by the labor unions.

He stomped into the office of his head engineer. "Mike, what is going on around here? Why aren't these people at their desk working?"

Mike looked up at him with vacant eyes. "Haven't you heard?" he asked.

"Heard what?" Devoe shouted, the uneasiness getting stronger.

"About the disappearances and the earthquakes," Mike whispered barely loud enough for Devoe to hear.

"Good Lord, man, of course I heard. What's that got to do with us here in Houston, Texas?" Devoe had little patience for weak men.

"Listen, we've faced bigger obstacles than what Mother Nature can inflict on us. Have you been in touch with our office in California? What about the European and Middle East offices?"

"Where are all our employees? Do they think this is a good time to call in sick? Is it a strike? A takeover attempt? Mike, Mike," he yelled at the man.

Mike didn't answer, a blank stare on his face. Devoe stormed out of the office.

He spent frenzied days trying to locate Joyce and other DCI employees. He hired investigators to uncover what plot was being set up to topple his domain. The fact that the outside world had been shocked by the mysterious disappearance of millions meant nothing to him. His own little world was all that mattered. The fact that his wife was gone meant nothing as well. She'd been threatening to leave him for years.

I won't just lie down and roll over, he thought after receiving yet another empty report from investigators. *I know too many government secrets. No one can push me aside.*

The Alliance Project is moving along nicely, he reflected. *The new DEA facilities are nearing completion, as well as my new private international airport. With my computer databases linking financial records, tax records, health records, pension records, property records, and drivers licenses on my state-of-the-art computer system, "they" can't afford not to have me around. Americans love me.*

He savored the recent information he'd received of the ground roots swell for his next presidential campaign.

The only good thing about this total chaos was that he no longer had to deal with Bob Wells.

Josh climbed into his limo thinking about Emily Wells' ridiculous accusation yesterday that the Republican Party had planned a coup and had kidnapped the president and killed the vice president.

We're really in for it now, he thought. *I'll have tons of material for the show.*

Even that acknowledgment didn't give him any pleasure. There was something stirring in his spirit, a nagging he couldn't quite pin down.

Josh would have been tempted to believe it all a hoax, except for the strange call he had received from his friend, Israeli Foreign Affairs Minister Benjamin Sadle.

Once the media informed the public of the mass catastrophes occurring around the world that Monday, Josh had stayed up late watching the news reports on CNN. At 5:00 a.m. he was jarred out of a restless sleep by the sound of the telephone.

"Hello," he growled.

"Josh, this is Ben Sadle. Please forgive me for waking you."

"Ben, what's going on?" Josh shook himself awake, knowing the call must be urgent.

"Josh, I don't know how to tell you this, but Itzak Bet was just found dead. He committed suicide." Ben's heart pounded in his chest. "I've been appointed prime minister."

"What?" Josh sat up in bed. "Why would Itzak commit suicide?"

"I don't know," Ben said. "He was a national hero after Israel soundly defeated the Russians and Arabs. The authorities are investigating it, but they've hit a major snag. They can't find Itzak's wife."

Josh was utterly astounded. Nothing that had happened in the last thirty-six hours made sense. "Do the authorities think she was kidnapped?" Josh asked.

"They're looking at that possibility," Ben said. "They discovered she was a member of a Messianic congregation. But," he coughed, "they've been unable to locate any members of the group."

"Wow," Josh said. "Congratulations on your new position, Ben."

"Thanks, but I would have preferred this to have happened under different circumstances."

"When will Israel hold new elections?" Josh asked, adjusting the bed covers.

"I'm not sure at this point if they will. Since the war ended, there have been mass demonstrations calling for the Messiah and the rebuilding of the Temple.

Josh and Ben heard loud crackling, breaking up what had been a clear connection between Jerusalem and New York.

"Josh...Josh."

The eerie sound of Ben's voice caused Josh to shiver with goosebumps.

"Josh, we've found the Ark." The line continued to crackle and pop.

"What, the real Ark? Like *Raiders of the Lost Ark*? Ben, are you sure? Ben?" Josh yelled into a dead line.

Josh hung up the phone and leaned back against the headboard. "This is getting too weird."

5

"Therefore, say to the house of Israel, 'Thus says the Lord God, "It is not for your sake, O House of Israel, that I am about to act, but for My holy name, which you have profaned among the nations where you went.
"And I will vindicate the holiness of My great name which has been profaned among the nations, which you have profaned in their midst. Then the nations will know that I am the Lord," declares the Lord God, "when I prove Myself holy among you in their sight.
For I will take you from the nations, gather you from all the nations."
(Ezekiel 36: 22-23) (NAS)

Tuesday's show started as usual with the exception of callers. In the seven years Josh had been broadcasting from New York, the popularity and notoriety of his show had skyrocketed to unchartable proportions.

A few minutes before show time Josh noticed his production staff whispering in the booth, as if they were trying to hide their conversation from him. He hit the microphone button. "What are you guys doing in there? Aren't we a little mature for gossip? And what's with the phones? Why aren't they lit up? Is there a problem with the equipment?

"I wouldn't doubt it after yesterday," he mumbled under his breath.

I should have stayed home. If people weren't counting on hearing my voice, the voice of reason and truth, I would have. He cursed his dedication.

As Josh started the monologue the phone board lit up, as did a smile on his face.

I haven't lost it yet, he thought to himself.

Josh went to his first caller. "Hello, Tim in Atlanta, Georgia, welcome to the Josh Cohen Show."

"Josh, thank goodness you're still here." Tim vibrated with excitement.

"Wah, of course I'm still here, Tim. You don't think I'd let an earthquake keep me from being your beacon of light, do you?" Josh questioned.

"Josh," Tim said, "I was afraid they'd gotten to you too!"

"What do you mean by that?"

"Haven't you heard of all the religious people who have been rounded up and detained in secret concentration camps?"

"Oh, come on. You don't really believe people of faith have been rounded up and taken to camps do you?" Josh expelled a loud sigh. "Emily isn't Hitler, and this isn't the same United States that rounded up the Japanese Americans after Pearl Harbor was bombed. "Tim," he asked, "can you hang on? I've got to take a commercial break."

"Sure," Tim agreed, excited to be on the phone with Josh Cohen.

"Les," Josh chastised his call screener, "why do you insist on putting through callers that are one card short of a full deck?"

"Josh, this is not going to be your kind of day. Every line I've got on hold is one bizarre story after another. What do you think of UFOs?"

"Oh, good grief! Don't you dare put someone like that on the air." Josh swore under his breath.

Les couldn't believe the weird calls. He'd never had crank callers with the kind of stories these people were telling. Men and women alike telling him of UFO sightings, alien abductions, vaporizations, stories about "mature souls" transcending this plane to a higher plane and are now channeling through those here on earth.

"What do you think of channeling?" Les asked his boss.

"What? Channeling? What on earth are you talking about?" Josh shook his head in amazement.

"You know, using a host to communicate the spirit's message through the caller to the world on your show."

"Pleease," Josh begged.

"Hey, man, I've even had a couple of callers claiming that Christ had raptured all the Christians."

"Oh, not again." Josh had heard that story before.

Les motioned for Josh the end of the commercial break.

"Okay, folks, we're back from the break. Tim, you still with us?" Josh asked.

"I'm here, Josh," Tim answered.

"Now let's get back to your assertion that religious folks have been rounded up and put in concentration camps."

"That's right, Josh. I have a report from Dr. Bruce Andrews of the Intelligence Digest Report which says that the United States has been divided into ten regional areas. Federal detention centers have been set up in Florida, Virginia, Georgia, Wisconsin, Arkansas, California, New York, Pennsylvania. and Arizona and have been placed under the direction of the United Nations," Tim explained.

"Tom." Josh sounded exasperated. "Supposedly all the disappearances happened around the same time. How do you think all these folks were kidnapped at the same time around the world by the United Nations, right from under the nose of family and friends?" Josh expelled his breath. "Now I'll give you your insistence of detention centers since you're reading from Intelligence Digest Report, but they must have been set up for a different purpose, because there is no human way that 'millions' of people could have been gathered together and transported from around the world to detention centers without anyone knowing about it.

"Even the liberal media wouldn't let a story like that get away, and besides, what about the alleged disappearance of Bob Wells? Do you think," Josh chuckled, "that Emily had Bob whisked away so she could take over the presidency?" Josh broke into a hearty laugh. "Now that's something to talk about. I knew she wanted his job, but I didn't think she would go to these lengths to get it. Thanks for calling, Tim. We'll be back. Don't go away, folks."

Josh cut to another commercial and leaned back in his chair. "Give me a break," he said. "I've had about as much of this malarkey as I can stand. What's wrong with these people."

"We're coming back on air, Josh. One, two, three," his production assistant shouted and pointed at Josh as the ON THE AIR green light flashed on.

"Folks, we're back, talking to people who think the world is coming to an end. Now let's try to get our feet planted on solid ground. I understand many of you have experienced terrible devastation due to the earthquakes, and I know everyone has their own story about where millions of people have disappeared to, but let's try to stay with the facts and stop all this speculation."

Josh read the board trying to decide which caller to take next. "Hello, Sarah from Clarksville, Tennessee."

"Josh, oh Josh, I can't believe I got through to you. I just love your show. With all this turmoil in the world, I don't know what I would have done if I'd turned on the radio today and you hadn't been here," Sarah went on breathlessly.

"Thank you, Sarah," Josh laughed. "Have no fear. Your beacon of light and voice of truth is here to guide you through the crazy days ahead." Josh warmed up to this caller. "Now, Sarah, tell us why you called."

"Josh..." Sarah's voice quivered. "My husband is one of the missing."

Josh dreaded this conversation already. "Sarah," he asked, "where do you think he has disappeared to?"

"Heaven," she said.

"Was he killed in the earthquake?" Josh asked hesitantly.

"No, I think Jesus came and took him to heaven."

Here we go again. "Sarah, why do you think Jesus came and got him and took him to heaven?"

"Well, my husband was a Christian. I'm Jewish." She paused for a moment. "Anyway, I found his Bible this morning, and when I picked it up, it opened to 1 Thessalonians 4. Verse 16 through 18 says, 'For the Lord himself will come down from heaven, with a loud command, with the voice of the archangel and with the trumpet call of God, and the dead in Christ will rise first. After that, we who are still alive and are left will be caught up with them in the clouds to meet the Lord in the air. And so we will be with the Lord forever. Therefore encourage each other with these words.'"

The air space became void, except for Josh's breathing into the microphone. That nagging feeling returned. Josh resisted it.

"Sarah, I'm sorry you can't find your husband, but I don't believe that God removed the Christians from the earth yesterday. After all, you and I are still here and we're God's chosen people. But just to prove it, I'm going to call my good friend and a Christian, Dave Malone. Matter of fact," Josh continued, "I'm going to call him right now. "Billy Joe," he hollered at his assistant producer. "BJ, you've got Dave's number in there. Get him on the line for me, please, and we'll clear up this mess right now about God taking the Christians. I can guarantee you, Sarah, that God didn't take the Christians and leave the Jews. After all, we are His chosen people. Thanks for your call, Sarah. We'll be right back, folks. Stay tuned for the last hour. Don't go away."

Josh barked at BJ, "Have you got Dave on the line yet?"

BJ shook his head. "There's no answer at his home, and his office hasn't seen him today. His secretary sounds like a basket case."

"Oh, that's just great," Josh said. "I've got to get hold of him before this show is over."

The recent disappearances, the attack on Israel by Russia and the Arab Coalition, and the horrible earthquakes caused Josh to think about the Almighty. He had scoffed privately at the "Religious Right" and their fundamentalist view of God.

"I don't believe," he'd insisted many times, "that a loving God would take some people and leave the rest here on earth to suffer." Even though he was Jewish, he had enjoyed a large following of Christian listeners; however, recent Nielsen ratings had revealed the loss of some twelve million people. He thought back at the times he had become irritated at a fanatic Christian caller.

He remembered accusing Les Diamond, his call screener, of putting the most radical Christians on the air just to annoy him. He recalled one lady who insisted that President Wells had pushed for the World Trade Alliance because it was what the Trilateral Commission wanted, and that Wells had been instructed by the CFR and TC to ensure its passage.

Josh had gotten himself worked up into a real lather and told her that the Trilateral Commission had nothing to do with it. Ford Devoe was a globalist and he opposed it. Josh insisted that people don't create opposing factions just to have balance.

"For example," he remembered saying, "God did not create Satan." There was a brief moment of silence before he went on to quickly add, "But I don't want to get into that discussion." Josh had quickly changed the subject. Theological discussions had no place on his program. He had regretted saying it. Every time he said something contrary to anyone's spiritual doctrine he caught all kinds of trouble for it. He didn't want to discuss the personal side of his beliefs because, as he told one religion reporter, "My radio show is not the place for that. I don't want to argue people's faith with them, and I don't want to get into arguments about the Bible."

Emily paused after reading her speech for the third time and looked at the flags displayed proudly on either side of her.

I do like sitting here, she thought. *I can't believe this is happening. I can't believe it was so easy. I don't know what they've done with Bob, but I hope they keep him.* She erupted into fits of giggles.

The blaring ring of the "red" phone startled Emily back to reality. She jumped up and grabbed the receiver. "Hello," she said timidly. "This is President pro tem Emily Wells."

"Emily, dear, this is Pope Simon Peter."

"Your Eminence, how nice of you to call." She frowned. Emily had met the pope at his induction ceremony, but as far as she knew, the pope and Bob hadn't had any contact since then. Emily had been raised a Methodist, but she rarely attended church since childhood. She'd gone with Bob a couple of times, usually for a photo opportunity while he was governor. Emily's parents had decided it wasn't worth enduring the tantrums to make her attend.

"Dear child," Simon Peter said, "I know what stress you must be going through with this right-wing conspiracy effort to gain control of the White House.

"Please be assured that you have my full support. Matter of fact, I'd consider it an honor if you'd let me come and bless the nation under your leadership until the president can be returned to his rightful position of authority.

"As I'm sure you've heard by now, God has chosen this particular time to send many intolerant Catholics to purgatory for purification. And it necessitates that I make a trip to the States to reassure and comfort the remaining cardinals and bishops for the heavy task ahead of them."

This was more than Emily could have hoped for. What better way to solidify her control in these uncertain times than to have the pope recognize her authority.

I'll take any support being offered. It might even be worth considering a conversion to Catholicism, she mused. Pope Simon Peter was well known for his political connections.

"Your Holiness," she whispered, as if the breath had been taken from her, "that would be wonderful."

"I'll arrange my schedule immediately," Simon Peter insisted.

"Thank you so much." Emily hung up, then dropped to the chair and sat in near amazement.

The girls aren't going to believe this stroke of luck. She reached for the phone to call her friend, confidant and Secretary of Health and Human Services Deane Shannon.

Simon Peter planned to accomplish much more on his trip to the United States than to just "bless" Emily's administration.

"Paul," he called for his secretary. "Have you confirmed my speech to the UN assembly yet?"

"I'm working on it, Your Eminence."

"You must remember, son, my destiny, my God-given authority is to reunite the true church under Mary—loving, kind, forgiving, gentle mother Mary."

He pondered a sudden thought. "Mother Mary, Mother earth, Mother nature, mother of change, mother of freedom, the mother church, mother goddess–all these are the same. I'll reunite the world under one accepted element: the element of mother, queen of heaven. You don't have to be religious to accept the connotation."

"No, sir," Paul agreed.

"Environmentalists will embrace Mother Earth; feminists will embrace the female element of mother; the oppressed will embrace freedom; the disenchanted will embrace change. Who better than 'Mother' to address the overpopulation of the earth and the social and environmental ills that plague her today?" Simon Peter smiled. "How do I do it?"

"I don't know, sir. It's awesome."

Harry took the service road to work Tuesday morning. The rapture had caused hazardous driving conditions and city services worked frantically to clear the roads. Texans had experienced only a minor tremor of the earthquakes, but the rapture had caused considerable damage.

The airports were national disasters. Around the world, planes engaged in takeoff and descent now littered the runways.

The FAA claimed the crashes were a result of some unexplainable atmospheric phenomenon. Experts were still trying to explain what happened to the crew and passengers who disappeared.

Harry got on the elevator and punched 7.

Well, I've got my ticket now, he thought. *Too bad I missed the first takeoff.*

The office whirled in pandemonium when he arrived at 7:30 that morning. Nearly everyone at the office had been affected in some manner by the events of the previous day, even though Austin hadn't sustained any damage to speak of. The TV in the breakroom tuned to CNN blared a rundown of the earthquakes and the catastrophes they created.

The death toll rose by the hour and rescue efforts were well underway. Destruction in the third world countries topped the chart. Fortunately, United States building codes in the last fifty years had prevented the same type of destruction Europe now experienced. However, the United States would be crippled for months and possibly years in some areas because of severe infrastructure damage. Buckled roads and highways, including the largest freeway in the world, located in Los Angeles, would cause long-term repercussions.

Downed bridges in San Francisco, Denver, St. Louis, Boston, New York, Dallas, and many other cities effectively crippled the economy and mobile public. Fires continued to blaze around the world, many caused by broken natural gas lines. Dams burst in many areas unleashing billions of pounds of pent-up water to rush unchecked, carrying along with it anything in its wake. Urgent inspections of U.S. and Russian nuclear plants had been underway since the first aftershocks began.

Harry was not a big Josh Cohen fan, but Kaye had enjoyed the program. Harry turned it on to see what Josh would say to listeners calling in about the rapture. *Josh is going to have a rude awakening,* Harry thought to himself.

On Friday, Josh walked into his office apprehensive about the show. It had been a horrible week for him. The callers were driving him nuts, and he was plagued by a nagging voice in the back of his mind. Something seemed to be meandering around up there, but the particulars eluded him. It irritated him that he couldn't shake the feeling. He thought about that first Tuesday of work following "Death Monday." He reflected on the chaos he'd observed all week from the backseat of his limo headed to the studio downtown. The streets were a war zone, and a large number of the victims appeared to be ascetic Jews.

He'd seen news reports of men being beaten to death, synagogues and cemeteries desecrated, and businesses bombed in the Jewish section of the city. It was as if someone had suddenly poured a full bottle of anti-Semitism out on the city of New York. The city had suffered the aftermath of the earthquakes. Major traffic accidents resulted from the idiots who had panicked and gotten out of their cars, leaving them running in the middle of the street. Bridges and buildings collapsed, and the shards of millions of broken windows rained down upon the streets below. But curiously, there were few reports of disappearances in New York City, quite unlike the stories from around the world.

6

"And one of the elders
saith unto me, weep not:
behold, the Lion of the
tribe of Judah the
Root of David, hath
prevailed to open the
book, and to loose the
seven seals thereof."
(Revelation 5:5)

In the months that followed "Death Monday," as it was called by the media, Harry spent hours at the public library researching all he could find concerning the Jews and Israel.

He knew the Jews were God's chosen people, but he hadn't ever paid much attention to the book of Daniel, until Kaye had insisted that the Jews had been appointed one final period of time, referred to as 'Jacobs 70th week,' to accept Jesus Christ as the Messiah.

Harry sat among the stacks in the periodical section of the library, searching through international newspapers and major U.S. papers. In his search he happened upon the November 8, 1949 issue, of the *Israeli News*. A bold headline spanned page one–"Operation Magic Carpet." The first sentence proclaimed, "Tens of thousands of Jews were taken in a dramatic operation from Yemen to Aden, and from there flown to Israel."

Harry continued looking through the newspapers for major news of Jewish immigration. He found an article about "Operations Ezra and Nehemiah" and one on "Operation Moses," a clandestine airlift in 1984 that relocated 12,000 Ethiopian Felashas until national broadcast of the operation brought Ethiopia under criticism from Arab neighbors, causing the government to halt the airlift. In 1989, he read further, the immigration of Ethiopian Jews continued at a rate of a few hundred a month in an exchange for arms.

Harry got up, stretched, and meandered to the water fountain. His muscles were sore from sitting so long. As he rounded the corner, he bumped into an attractive woman in her mid to late thirties.

"Pardon me," he said and bent down to help her retrieve the books he'd knocked out of her arms. The fragrant scent that floated up from her hair as she knelt beside him caused a sudden longing. Harry picked up a book and noticed the title, "Bible Prophecy, A Sign of the Times" by Charlie Klause. "Interested in Bible prophecy?" Harry asked.

She gave him a wary glance, and Harry couldn't help but notice the long dark lashes that framed her big green eyes.

"Why do you ask?" She tensed, seeing in Harry a strong resemblance to her ex-husband.

Harry realized he hadn't introduced himself. "I'm Harry Levine. Please forgive me for being curious. I've been studying Bible prophecy these last few months, and I'm just surprised to find someone else doing the same thing."

"I'm sorry." She relaxed, feeling silly for her suspicion. "My name is Marilyn Stahl. You can't be too careful these days," she joked half seriously.

"I know what you mean," Harry agreed. "My world has certainly been turned upside down."

Harry helped her carry the books to a table and they sat down. The late afternoon sun filtered through the windows as the library emptied.

"Did you lose your wife?" Marilyn blurted out. "Oh…" She quickly covered her mouth. "I'm sorry. I shouldn't have asked such a personal question. It just popped out."

"It's okay," he said. "I'm divorced. But I lost...good friends." Harry stared down at the table, afraid she would read the pain in his eyes. "But," he said, "I'll see them all again."

Marilyn reached over and placed her hand over his. "You're a believer?"

Harry lifted his head, a smile spread across his face. "Yes. Unfortunately, it took the rapture to open my eyes. I don't know what it is that kept me from seeing all the signs."

"I know." Marilyn quickly looked down to hide the tears. Harry reached over and placed his other hand over hers.

She looked up and wiped a tear from her check.

Harry squeezed her hand.

She sniffed and let out a little laugh.

Harry found himself soaking in the first deep emotion he had shared with another in months. His feelings welled up in a desperate attempt to hang on to it.

"It's getting late. Would you like to go get a bite to eat?" Harry nervously rushed on without waiting for an answer. "There aren't many places still open to eat, and it's not kosher, but I know of a little deli not far from here. We have a remnant who gather for fellowship and Bible study. Would you like to meet them?"

"I'd love something as normal as eating and laughing with friends." She smiled at Harry. "The last meal I ate out turned my stomach. I thought discovering my husband's infidelity was bad. We divorced soon after." She rolled her eyes. "Ha, and I thought things could only get better."

Driving to the restaurant, they discussed the depressing spirit that had settled over their workplaces after the Christians had been taken. Marilyn told Harry how she and her best friend, Pam, who had recently committed suicide, used to make fun of one of the men in their office.

"We used to say he was president of the God Squad," Marilyn said. "Now I wish we had listened to him instead of making fun of him."

Harry slowly turned into a dark parking lot in front of an old run-down building. Broken glass lay on the curb at the foot of the streetlight.

The building was boarded up halfway. BB holes dotted the exposed glass above. The downtown neighborhood looked deserted.

Marilyn felt a moment's anxiety as Harry came around and opened her door. A cold burst of wind chilled her face. Harry offered his hand. She hesitated, pulling her suit jacket closer. The seconds passed by.

Why am I in downtown Austin, Texas, sitting in a car in front of a trashed-out building with no lights with a man I don't even know? She looked up into his face and held her hand out.

His grasp was warm and reassuring. Still she shuddered as they approached a plain board door covered with gang writing. Harry pushed a small bell. A gust of wind whipped around the building, stirring trash and leaves in the empty parking lot. Weeds growing out of the cracks in the concrete grabbed at Marilyn's skirt. She leaned closer to Harry and studied his back, admiring his broad shoulders.

Keys were inserted into the lock from the inside and a bar was lifted. The door cracked opened. "Can I help you?" a man asked.

"Tommy, it's me. Harry." The door opened just enough to let them in.

"Hey, old friend, long time no see." Tommy slapped Harry on the back.

"Still lifting weights, Tommy?" Harry grimaced and then laughed. "This is Marilyn."

"Nice to meet you, Marilyn." Tommy locked the door behind her. "Come on back."

They followed Tommy through a dark dining hall. Tables were scattered about with chairs stacked on top. A dim light shining from the back lit the way. The sound of Marilyn's high heels echoed off the cold tile floor.

Several people sitting around a kitchen table looked up as they came through the door.

"Gang," Tommy said, "this is Harry's friend, Marilyn. That's Janet, Stan, Kevin, Donna, and Sally. There's always a group of us here," he said. "The faces change but the reason we gather is always the same."

"Do you know the Messiah?" asked the dark-haired girl introduced as Janet.

"Yes," Marilyn answered shyly.

Tommy moved two more chairs up to the table. "Interested in something to eat?" Tommy asked.

"Whatever you've got," Marilyn said, unsure what to say. Since the president's disappearance and Emily's assuming the office, prices had skyrocketed and food had become a valued commodity. Few select restaurants were still open. Only the governmental elite continued business as usual.

Tommy set down two plates of steamed vegetables.

"This is the largest gathering of Jews I've seen in a while," Marilyn said as picked up her spoon.

Donna giggled.

"Hum...I guess you're right, Marilyn. I hadn't really thought about it," Tommy mused.

"So, how did y'all come to the Messiah?" Marilyn looked around at each of them.

"In different ways," Tommy said. "Strange as it may sound, the Lord sent me a messenger, and I spread the word around to those of my customers who came back after the rapture. Some believed me and some didn't." Tommy shrugged.

Marilyn studied the faces of the people around her. She admired Sally's peaches and cream complexion, her long curly auburn hair, and her infectious laugh.

Donna was just the opposite—petite, olive-complexioned, and quiet.

Kevin had his arm gently around her. A backpack dangled carelessly from the back of Kevin's chair, indicating he and Donna were probably students at "the" university, one of the last places of higher education in Texas that hadn't closed down.

Marilyn listened intently as Stan's baritone voice filled the small room with the story of the latest case of harassment by law enforcement.

The media had recently started portraying Jews as subversive, anti-community, anti-unity troublemakers. Harassment of Jews and believers alike had become a common occurrence. Even law-abiding citizens had been made to feel afraid.

"Jews are responsible for the world's woes. Just like Hitler said," Stan smirked.

Once Emily enacted FEMA and Executive Order 12148, her cabinet created a new department of the government that incorporated all city services such as police and various public service departments like fire and emergency services into it.

She eagerly embraced the new department at the suggestion of the Attorney General Joni Rains. Its main objective was to search for the president, find the vice president's killer, and to round up suspected participants of the coup.

The SSS–Joni and Emily jokingly called the Secret Search for Saints because of the ridiculous claims that the president had been raptured–was under the Armed Service division of the United States government. It replaced all municipal protection services. Individual autonomous police departments no longer existed. Everything was now under one authority: Emily's.

In the weeks that followed Emily's ascent to power, Josh blasted her on the show and raved against her forming the SSS. He had given his show over weekly to conservative congressmen and senators as a platform to alert the public and expose what Emily had done.

As the weeks passed and Josh was unable to sway public opinion into voicing outrage over Emily's enactment of Executive Order 12148, he began to grow detached and listless. It was as if the root of conservatism had been removed. Liberalism was running rampant, and not even Josh Cohen could impact it.

Josh twisted and swiveled, fidgeting in his chair as the show began.

"Folks, you'll have to excuse me," he pleaded. "I'm a little scatterbrained today. My mind is on other things." He rattled his papers. "But I realize you people have come to count on me to be solid, dependable, reliable.

"I'm not allowed the normal reaction to distractions, inattentiveness and the 'I just don't want to be here' days, which most people experience," he bemoaned.

"It's just that—I can't believe we have allowed a woman to come in and take over the country. And I can't believe there's still so many unanswered questions–like, why hasn't the body of President Wells been found?

"Whoa, you know I'm upset when I'm anxious to find Bob Wells.

"But besides Wells, where are all those people who left their cars on the freeway? And, why weren't the bodies of airline pilots and half the passengers found at all the crash sites?

"I tell you, folks. Someone has got to get to the bottom of all this. Don't go away. Back in a moment."

Josh dragged himself out of bed and stumbled to the bathroom. It had gotten harder and harder to get up in the mornings and go to work. What once had been the most exciting part of his life had now become the most dreaded.

The audience had changed, the country had changed, the world had changed, and he couldn't fight it any longer. The desire to be right was gone. Fear had taken its place. A large part of his audience switched to Levi Steiner, the obnoxious, filthy, loudmouth talk-radio host who shouted obscenities and entertained his listeners by cussing out and hanging up on "stupid callers." Steiner delighted in discussing lewd topics and shocking the audience with his ribald comments and opinions.

Josh looked at himself in the mirror as he shaved. His eyes were bloodshot from weeks of lack of sleep. He had dropped twenty-five pounds in the last month. The inability to locate his friend Dave Malone had taken its toll. His days had been spent struggling through the rigors of preparing and airing his daily radio talk show. His nights were spent tossing and turning, searching for the sleep that evaded him.

As he glided the razor across his cheekbones, he noticed the lack of life in his eyes. Suddenly the stress and pressure of the last couple of months came crashing down. Large tears formed and rolled down, one by one, until streaks stained his cheeks.

The flood gates opened, and Josh fell on his face seeking the Almighty. *Okay, okay...I'll stop running. I can't go on. I don't have the answers. Please, God.*

He grew up in a typical Jewish family. He had faithfully attended synagogue, practiced most of the feasts and did what good modern Jews did. But he couldn't remember the last time he had attended synagogue or even talked with a rabbi.

Somehow he managed to get dressed. When he walked out of the elevator, Charlie, his doorman, hurried to open the door. The limo driver shut the car door after he slid into the back.

"I need a synagogue, James," he told the driver. "Stop at the first one you see."

It wasn't hard to spot. Graffiti and hateful words desecrated the beautiful building. Josh slipped through the front entrance, surprised the door was unlocked. Light forced its way through stained-glass windows and dimly illuminated the empty lobby.

He reached for the doors leading into the sanctuary and subconsciously searched the top of his head.

God, forgive me, but I don't have a yarmulke to cover my head with today, and I don't think we have time for me to go find something.

The strange calm that filled the room was a radical change from the world outside. He sat down in a pew and studied the large ornate gold menorah at the front. *Well, I'm here. What now?*

"Hello, may I, hel... wha... you're Josh Cohen," the startled rabbi said as Josh looked up.

Josh jumped up. "Oh, Rabbi, you startled me."

"I'm sorry. I haven't had many visitors show up and quietly sit down. Most are rushing in seeking protection from the violence outside."

"Well, in a way I am. I need refuge from this horrible, nagging feeling in my gut that won't go away."

The rabbi nodded in understanding. "Oh, that. Yes, I know what you're talking about." The rabbi sat down in the pew beside him.

"You've got it too?" Josh adjusted his position to get a better look at the rabbi's face. Radio training enabled him to gain insight into his callers from their voice inflection. But the real lessons had come from the hard knocks of life schooling him in reading body language.

"Yep," he nodded his head. "At first, when all the Christians disappeared, I thought it was just stress causing my stomach to act up. But..." He sighed. "I soon realized it was the truth of the Gospel that I was running from."

Josh gripped the back of the pew in front of him with his right hand. "But, Rabbi, you can't be saying–Rabbi, we're the chosen people. We've got a covenant with God."

"Yes, we're God's chosen people; and, yes, we have a covenant with God. But we proved we couldn't keep our part of the covenant. God made a new covenant to provide for our salvation, and to fulfill the first one. It's time we accepted it."

Josh stared at him. His brain doubted the rabbi's words, but his heart was breaking inside.

He bowed his head. The rabbi placed his hand on Josh's shoulder and began to pray. "O Lord God Almighty, I beseech you to look down upon the sons of Israel. We have sinned. We come before you in repentance. Have mercy upon us. Have mercy upon thy servant Josh Cohen. Open his eyes, O Lord God."

As Josh bowed his head, the rabbi's words washed over him, breaking down the walls of excuses he had built over the years. Wrongs he had thought long forgotten broke through his conscience, and he began to sob and ask for God's mercy and forgiveness. He submitted himself to the Lord, and a deep peace descended and filled the emptiness inside him. Lines that had scarred his brow for months faded away. An unexplained energy pumped through his veins. As he looked up, he felt a new, urgent purpose for his life.

"Thank you," he said to the rabbi, a gentle knowing shining in his eyes.

"Go in peace. He will guide you now in these troubled times," the rabbi said.

Josh nodded his head in understanding and then silently left the synagogue. Slipping into the limo, the driver closed his door, and soon they were heading downtown.

He bounced into the studio.

"What happened to you?" BJ asked in surprise.

"I met my Maker this morning." The smile on his face stretched his cheek muscles to the limit.

BJ and Les looked at each other and shook their heads. "All this has really gotten to him," Les whispered.

Josh sat down at his desk and collected the headlines of the few remaining publications. He formulated his thoughts and what he wanted to say in today's monologue. The excitement grew as show time approached.

7

"Arise, shine;
for thy light is come,
and the glory of the Lord
is risen upon thee."
(Isaiah 60:1)

Harry and Marilyn arrived at Tommy's Cafe in time for the Josh Cohen Show. Tommy usually had it on during the noon hour, and they had gotten in the habit of going there for lunch. They entered through the back door, unbolted during the day for the few friends who still dropped by.

Marilyn noticed several people she'd met the other night. Donna and Kevin sat in the corner, taking a break from class.

Janet, wearing an attractive dark suit and matching shoes, occupied a table near the door to the closed dining hall.

A radio news announcer finished the top of the hour news. "I'm Robin Simms and this is 1550 AM. Stay tuned next for the Josh Cohen Show."

Marilyn drummed her thumb on the table, keeping beat with the theme song.

"You are now listening to a special edition of the Josh Cohen Show," the announcer said.

Josh took a deep breath. "Welcome, good brothers and sisters."

Harry and Marilyn looked at each other, surprised. Josh had never addressed his audience as brothers and sisters.

"Today is a special day and we are going to search out the truth together. We'll take a break and be back right after this."

"Do you suppose..." Marilyn hesitated, her eyes lighting up as she straightened her back and scooted to the edge of her chair.

"Do I suppose Josh has become a believer?" Harry finished her question, eager himself for affirmation from Josh.

"We're back, folks. Hold on to your hats because I'm getting ready to take you on a ride you won't forget," Josh said. "I now know where approximately one-third of the world's population has disappeared to. That's right, folks, I'm going to enlighten you. Yes, me, Josh Cohen, previously in the dark, but now in the light. And for sharing this information with you, I will be criticized, hounded, investigated, and persecuted... but it's worth it. Don't go away. Back after this."

"You're listening to the Democracy in Action Network," the announcer said as they broke for another commercial.

"I don't believe it," Harry said. Tommy served their soup and sandwich and pulled up a chair.

"What do you think, Tommy?" Marilyn asked. "Sounds like Josh has found the Lord, and probably a whole bunch of trouble to go with it."

"Welcome back, folks," Josh said with a laugh. "You wouldn't believe the calls that have flooded our phone lines and the crazy theories that we've been deluged with. Folks, just quit guessing. I'm about to tell you where your loved ones have gone, but first I'm going to address Emily's accusation that the Christian Right attempted a takeover and that they plotted to kidnap and kill the president and vice president of the United States.

"Now, we've heard sworn testimony from top religious leaders that they had nothing to do with any disappearance of the president," Josh explained. "We've heard of the suicides that have plagued both parties. There's still no hint as to the whereabouts of the missing House and Senate members from both parties. The attorney general's recently formed SSS has come up empty-handed in its investigation of both parties, even in light of the harsh and cruel treatment we've heard from those under investigation.

"Soooo," Josh questioned, "was the disappearance of the president and the death of the vice president a plot by the Christian Right to take control of the government?" He paused to build the suspense. "I contend, no! Back in a minute," he said and went to another commercial.

"Harry," Marilyn said astounded, "I can't believe what I'm hearing. Doesn't Josh know that in this climate he's sealing his doom?"

Harry shook his head and took a sip of water.

Marilyn put her spoon down. "The Wells administration has been out to get rid of him ever since it came to the White House, and now he's giving them a reason." Marilyn moaned.

"From what Stan has said, the SSS is dealing with most true believers harshly," Harry interjected.

Janet couldn't help but overhear their conversation. She finished her salad and walked over to their table to pay Tommy. "I don't know why you insist on listening to that bigot," she charged. "All he does is criticize people who are different."

"Janet," Tommy said surprised, "you come in here for lunch all the time. I didn't know you had a distaste for Josh Cohen."

"Well, I do, but this is the closest place to the capitol building and the only thing left open around here. And since I'm usually reading a brief, I ignore the radio," she lied.

Marilyn wondered at Janet's outburst. As the show resumed, she quickly dismissed Janet's objections.

Emily despised talk radio. She also despised people who canceled lunch appointments at the last minute. The thought of going on down to the dining room wasn't appealing.

I'm not hungry anyway.

She paced the floor in what she now considered her office and noticed a radio. She turned it on.

"The opinions of this host make more sense than anyone else out there, and that is why millions of people are now listening to this show from afar." The voice of Josh Cohen echoed around the room.

Emily cursed under her breath. She hated that man. The door burst open and the attorney general rushed in. Emily's eyes narrowed as she glared at Joni, ready to blast her for the lack of respect permeating the White House lately.

"Emily, you've got to turn on the Josh Cohen Show. He's telling the world that he knows where Bob is," Joni shrieked. Emily's facial expression changed from fury to horror.

About that time Joni heard the radio in the background and realized Emily had it on. "Did you hear him?" she asked.

"No, I just turned it on." They stopped talking as the show resumed.

"Folks, the ship came in but I missed it. If you're hearing this broadcast, you missed it, too," Josh said. "And what I'm about to tell you just blows my mind. I can't get over the fact that Bob Wells made the cut. The blood covered even him." An audible sigh escaped over the airwaves.

Emily tensed, waiting for Josh to explain.

"I've always told you people," Josh continued, "if I'm wrong about something, I'll be the first to correct the error. You'll not be able to accuse me of spreading false information," he assured them. "If you'll recall the program the Tuesday following *Death Monday*, I had a caller who insisted the Christians had been raptured."

Josh looked up and saw the look of disbelief on the faces of his assistant producer and call screener.

"Les, her name was Sarah, wasn't it?" Josh asked.

Les nodded his head in agreement.

"Sarah from Clarksville, Tennessee, I believe," Josh added. "Well, Sarah said her husband was a Christian, and she said she'd been reading his Bible that morning and happened upon Matthew 24:37, which she claimed explained all the disappearances. And if you'll remember," he said, "I told her I'd put an end to that thought process by calling the most Christian man I knew—my friend Dave Malone. Well, dear friends, I never found Dave. Don't go away, we've got to take a quick break."

Had Josh been in his old state of hopelessness, he would have felt the suffocating presence of evil that descended upon the studio; but instead, he beamed with joy.

Emily couldn't believe her ears. "Do you realize what he just said," she shouted at Joni.

Joni was bewildered. People who talked in riddles flustered her. Emily exploded into a frenzied attack of hysterics.

"How dare Josh Cohen tell the world that Bob Wells has been raptured. Bob, who couldn't let a pretty face go by without getting her name and more. Bob, who thought the rich were crooks, yet wanted more than anything the things that money bought. Bob, who had no absolutes, no values. Bob, who said he gave his life to Christ at age eight but, at age forty-eight, acted no different from anyone else in Washington D.C."

Emily frantically searched her memory for anything that would point to evidence indicating Bob could have been raptured. The words of his deceased mother spoken in a conversation after their marriage popped into her head.

"I remember how excited Bob was about his so-called experience. I never took much stock in it personally. I felt he was just seeking an escape from the stress of living with an abusive alcoholic. I'll admit life with Bob's stepfather was a strain on all of us. To appease Bob I attended his baptism in that three-room building they called a church. I'll never forget the glow on that boy's face as he came up out of the water. I hated for him to be disillusioned later, so I didn't encourage him in that direction. I thought his stepfather would kill him when Bob came home one Sunday afternoon with some story those church people had obviously pushed on him that he'd been called into the ministry. After that incident, I did everything to keep him away from church folks.

"A couple of Sundays I forgot to wake him up in time; and with several weekend trips to the capitol that kept us out of town on Sunday, I eventually was able to steer him away from the ministry and into politics.

"I can't tell you what a thrill it was for me when Bob came home from a class trip to Washington, D.C., telling about his chance meeting with the president of the United States. That boy walked on clouds for weeks. The gods were smiling on us that day."

Emily relaxed. Even his mother knew better than to succumb to the brainwashing of the religious right of her day. Emily suddenly thought of Pope Simon Peter.

He is coming to bless my administration. She sighed with relief. *The pope is still here. Nobody went to heaven in some mysterious rapture.*

"Joni," she screeched, wondering what the woman was doing still standing in her office, "get that kook off the air."

"We already tried to by reenacting the Fairness Doctrine. It was voted down in Congress, remember."

"What is wrong with you people around here?" Emily screamed. "I enacted Executive Order 12148. I have the power to take over all communication media. Get him off now! Terri," Emily yelled at her secretary, "get the pope on the phone and schedule his trip immediately."

Emily plopped down in her chair and stared out the window. *I'm surrounded by idiots.*

Josh finished the radio program and headed to the advertising department. He eagerly greeted everyone he passed. It wasn't unusual for the young secretaries who occupied the glass cubicles to stop work long enough to watch the famous man walk by.

His executive producer, Steve Benson, stuck his head out the door. "Josh, do you have a minute?"

"Sure, Steve."

"Come on in." Steve walked around to his desk. "Have a seat."

"What's up? You don't look so good." Josh plopped down in a chair. The silence grew heavy.

"Come on, Steve, nothing can be that bad." Josh thumbed his fingers on his leg.

Steve took a deep breath and said, "I've just gotten off the phone with our attorneys."

"That doesn't sound too good. Rarely does good news come via an attorney. So what is it, Steve? Spit it out."

"I had an unexpected visit 30 minutes ago from the SSS Department...and they've canceled your show." Steve fiddled with a thread on his pants leg.

"They've what?" Josh shouted, jumping out of his chair. "They can't do that....on what grounds?" He pounded his fist on Steve's desk.

"They claim you're secretly communicating with the terrorist group responsible for the president's disappearance." Steve shook his head.

"Give me a break," Josh shouted. "No one kidnapped that sorry you-know-what." He was incredulous. "I can't believe the SSS thinks I had anything to do with Bob Wells. It galls me to think that Bob got raptured and I, Josh Cohen, didn't."

Steve had heard Josh allude to something of the sort on his program, but he hoped it was a joke.

The guy really does need a break, Steve decided.

"Josh, I've got our attorneys doing everything possible to combat the Attorney General's office. We've already filed an injunction with the District Judge and should hear something tomorrow."

"This isn't the end, Steve. This isn't the end," Josh said as he walked back to the control room. The bounce in his step was gone.

BJ and Les were still there preparing for the next day's program.

"What's up, boss?" BJ asked, surprised to see him back and surprised to see his smile gone already.

"We've been canceled, guys," Josh uttered, not wanting to rehash it all. "They won't get rid of me that easy. We're going to tape several different public service announcements along with a notice that the program has been moved. I want our listeners to raise such a ruckus demanding to know where we've moved the program that the White House will go nuts trying to find out as well.

"Where are we going to move it to?" Les asked.

After a long pause, Josh said, "I don't know yet."

It rained all night and well into the morning. Josh didn't wake up the usual time. The gentle patter of rain created an atmosphere too peaceful to rouse him from the oblivion of sleep with no alarm clock set to screech out its presence.

Josh woke just in time to switch on the radio and listen to the announcement Les and B.J. had prepared the day before.

"This is WABC Radio. I'm Kathy Spiegel and it's 11:05. Stay tuned for the Josh Cohen Show."

The anticipation of the introduction song brought a smile to his face. "They're coming to take me away ha-ha, they're coming to take me away hee-hee...," the announcement began. "Greetings, brothers and sisters. They have indeed come to take me away, but do not despair. I told you, when the powers that be tried to reenact the Fairness Doctrine again last year, I'm not going to go away, not even an executive order is going to get rid of me. If I have to, we'll set up in the middle of the Atlantic, buy our own satellite, and beam into your homes. Maybe even Ford Devoe will help us with the technology. In the meantime, don't be taken in by the darkness. I'll be back!" The theme song faded into the background and the replacement program took over.

I bet those phone lines are going crazy, Josh thought, delighted at himself.

Josh jumped when the phone rang. "Hello."

"Josh, this is Ben Sadle."

"Ben, good friend, what's going on?"

"What's all this I hear about you being taken off the air?"

"Where are you, Ben? It's the middle of the night in Jerusalem."

"I'm in Washington, Josh, but never mind that. What's happening to your program?"

"Can you believe it," Josh said. "The SSS, that new department Emily and Joni Rains, the attorney general, formed to hunt coup members forced the station to pull my program. And it wouldn't surprise me if Ford Devoe didn't have something to do with it as well."

"How can they get away with it?" Ben asked.

"Ben, under FEMA the powers that be control the media. There's nothing I can do about it."

"Have you made other arrangements for the program?"

"To tell you the truth, Ben, this all hit so fast that I'm still swimming in disbelief."

"Would you be interested in possibly bringing the show to Israel?"

"To Israel! Wow... Ben, that's something I've never thought about."

"It may sound like a crazy idea, but I've been hoping for something like this to happen for a long time. We need someone like you over here, Josh. We can set it up so that the signal can bounce off one of our satellites to the U.S., and listeners could pick it up on their shortwave radios."

"I'm really flattered, Ben. Can you give me a couple of days to think about it?"

"No problem, Josh. I'll wait to hear back from you. Take care, my friend."

Josh hung up the phone.

Wow! This is great, he thought. *I'd get to be in the very thick of things as the world as we know it draws to an end.*

The flight from the Vatican to New York had been rough. Simon hated to fly, but this was one opportunity he wouldn't miss for the world.

He was thrilled with himself. He'd been trying for days to formulate the right plan to bring peace to the war-torn Middle East. He wondered if he would be the one to bring the plan into action or if another would be chosen.

He appeared before the general assembly, tall and radiant in his white vestment, his dark curly hair sneaking out from under his tiara.

"Ladies and gentlemen, leaders and advisors of world governments, thank you for permitting me to speak before this assembly today." He scanned his notes. "You are gathered here today to formulate your course of action regarding Israel and her neighbors."

Muslims from Russia, India, Turkey, Africa, and the Arab states grew angry at his audacity. They grumbled among themselves.

"I have received a vision," Simon Peter said. A murmur ran through the assembly.

The pope quickly continued, "A vision from the God of the universe. The instructions I received were to tell the people of the world to reconcile themselves to their Muslim brothers, and for Israel to rebuild the Temple one hundred feet north of the Dome of the Rock. This is to be a sign to all the nations that He is the God of the Jews, the God of the Muslims, and the God of all religions and all faiths." He paused to let his words sink in. "You may ask why I was the recipient of a vision. I asked that very question myself and was told, as confirmation, that others would receive the same vision. Emily Wells has confirmed that she received a message through her spiritual guide, giving the same instructions."

The room burst into an uproar.

The next day all over the country headlines read, "Pope Receives Vision," "Israel Commanded to Rebuild Temple 100 north of Dome of Rock," and the "World to Unite Under One Faith." "All Religions Unite Under World Church." When interviewed, Islamic guru Sheik Hafez Nidal acknowledged, "Allah has spoken to me. Islamic faithful will pledge their allegiance by submitting to His servant Pope Simon Peter, the head of the newly formed World Church of Everlasting Peace."

Friday night rolled around and the small group now calling themselves the remnant arrived at Tommy's. It was Sally's turn to act as hostess, and she had baked a large chocolate cake. Lemon squares decorated a large platter garnished with lemon slices.

Everyone gathered around Stan's long coffee table with coffee and goodies. Their Bibles were scattered around the floor in easy reach.

"What do you think of all this special revelation stuff the pope talked about?" Marilyn asked, setting down her coffee cup.

"Well," Tommy said, "it means that Israel will rebuild the Temple, and the One World Religion referred to in Revelation 13 is being formed."

"Just tell me what's wrong with Muslims, Christians, and Jews putting aside their differences and coming together for the good of all? And why are you picking on the pope?" Janet challenged.

"Janet, that's a good question." Tommy couldn't believe his ears. He thought their Bible study had been more productive than that. "We've been getting together all these months to study Bible prophecy and to know what the Word says will happen during the tribulation period, and how we as believers are to respond to it. I'm not picking on the pope. The Christians went to heaven in the rapture. Obviously, the current pope is not a Christian. That doesn't mean other popes weren't Christians.

"Sally, read Revelation 13 and let's see what the Scripture says about the One World Religion."

"You know"–Marilyn put her Bible down when Sally finished reading–"this reminds me of something Josh Cohen talked about last year when Bob Wells went to Brussels for the NATO Summit."

"Oh, please." Janet slammed her Bible shut. "Do you have to bring Josh Cohen into our Bible study, too?"

"I'm sorry you don't like him, Janet," Marilyn apologized, "but he does base his show on current events, and they are lining up right now with the Scriptures."

Tommy interrupted their squabble. "So what were you saying, Marilyn?"

Collecting her thoughts and hoping not to offend Janet, Marilyn said, "Well, the big push was to allow as many countries, even the Warsaw Pact countries, to be a part of the North American Treaty Organization. The consensus was that with the destruction of communism in Russia, the Cold War was over and the members of NATO no longer need fear the Russians. Therefore, there was no longer a need for the protection of the United States. Now Josh's question to his listeners was what NATO member nation did we think would take the place of the U.S., not only a nation that would supply an adequate military force, but a nation that would take a lead role in the political policies and economic stability of Europe?"

"That's interesting," Harry said, "and scary when you think of Germany's history of anti-Semitism."

"Yeah," Stan said. "It makes you wonder if Hitler's regime was a foreshadowing of the Great Tribulation."

"It makes it easy to see why God would have allowed someone like Bob Wells in the presidency," Donna piped in. "It would take a man who was opposed to war to decrease our military strength in Europe from 350,000 to 100,000, a socialist who wanted to make everyone equal by taxing the American wealth away, and a man who thought the government was formed to solve the country's social ills instead of defending its liberty. What he has done, very effectively, I think"–Donna took a deep breath–"is to remove the United States as a world leader or world power, making way for the Antichrist to rise out of the revived Roman Empire."

Janet sulked the rest of the evening, refusing to participate in the discussion. *I'm not coming back,* she thought. *They're all weird. Josh Cohen, ugh!*

The Friday night Bible study had lost its appeal after the argument over Josh Cohen. Janet's thoughts turned to John Stadt. She thought about his cute smile, straight white teeth, and neatly trimmed blond beard she had admired the day he finally came over to her in the capitol dining room joking, "We've got to stop meeting like this."

Their flirtation soon budded into a romance. John was just what Janet needed. Someone interested in her and what was going on in her life instead of what was happening on the world scene.

Janet tried to focus on her work, but instead stared out the window. *Wish I could call Mom and tell her about my new love. I wish they hadn't insisted on retiring in California. They'd probably be alive today.* A moan threatened to escape. *Wish I had a life besides work and Tommy's goofy Bible study!*

"Hi, slim," John said, walking into Janet's office.

"Hi." she turned away from the window and smiled, her pulse beginning to race. "What brings you to my part of the world late Friday afternoon?"

"I had to bring a file to Congressman Williams. Thought I'd stop in to see if you wanted to have dinner? Or do you have plans to join your 'end of the world' friends tonight?" He taunted her, knowing she'd been offended at something they had said.

"No, I don't plan to join them tonight," she retorted.

"What do they talk about anyway?" John toyed with a pencil on her desk.

"They just read the Bible and talk about the Tribulation years ahead." Janet admired the way his dark tweed jacket set off his blond hair.

"What are the," he motioned, "quote, 'Tribulation' years?" John was curious about what her odd friends believed.

"I'm not clear on everything," she faltered at his intensity, "but it's the creation of a oneworld government and a oneworld religion, the loss of freedom, terrible persecution of Jews, plagues and ecological destruction, and the outpouring of God's wrath on the world."

"Good grief! It sounds like the religious right is overreacting to the ravings of fundamental fanatics."

"Oh no." Janet frowned. "They're just studying the Bible and discussing how best to endure the judgment that God will inflict on unrepentant sinners."

"Well, it sounds radical to me." John straightened a stack of papers on the corner of her desk. "You better stay clear just in case they get in trouble with the law. There's a new hate law on the books, you know."

Janet got up from her desk and approached him. "You think I don't know what new laws are on the books?"

John laughed. "I just love it when your eyes do that. What I'm trying to say is that I wouldn't want to lose you so soon after I found you." He reached around and began massaging her shoulders. "You're tense. You need a night out to loosen up."

Janet's heart pounded. She felt a flush redden her face. *How could I be so lucky*, she wondered. *Too bad Mom's not here to meet him.*

"I'll be back in an hour," he said. "We'll drop your car off and take mine. See ya soon." He winked and turned to go.

"Okay," she said, admiring his trim physique as he walked to the door.

When he returned, they left the capitol building and strolled a block to the parking garage. Janet pulled her coat tight, feeling the chill of a cold front.

John put his arm around her and squeezed. "You fit just right."

Janet savored her first real happiness in months, until she noticed three men standing by her car. Fear swept over her. "Are you Janet Mortz?" one man asked, flashing a badge.

"Yes," she squeaked, leaning against John.

"Open your trunk," he demanded.

"What for?" she cried. Janet couldn't believe this was happening. She remembered Stan, at Bible study, telling stories of normal citizens being hassled; but she thought he was exaggerating and hadn't paid much attention to them.

"This is a court order to search your trunk for 'hate crime' materials." He waved the paper in her face.

"That's ridiculous," Janet yelled, terror rising in her chest.

"Hold on a minute." John walked over to the man in charge. "I'm John Stadt, and I'm an SSS member. You've made a mistake." John pulled out a card and handed it to him.

The man who had been talking scanned it and passed it to one of his companions. "We're sorry to have bothered you, Ms. Mortz. It seems our information was incorrect. Please accept our apologies." He returned John's card. The men got in a dark blue Ford sedan and disappeared.

"What's going on?" Anger replaced Janet's fear.

"I warned you about hanging around with those 'end times' friends of yours." John shoved his wallet back into his inside jacket pocket.

"Those friends of mine haven't done anything wrong," Janet said with a voice louder than normal. "Besides, I haven't seen them in a couple of weeks." She put her hands on her hips. "Don't change the subject, John Stadt. I want to know what kind of card that is."

"It's my SSS card. All Masons have one." John took her keys and opened the door.

"So, what is it? What does it mean? What does it entitle you to?" She wasn't going to let this slip by as she had several other things lately.

"Get in," John said, handing her the keys. "Let's get out of here. I'll explain it later."

8

"Woe to you who desire the day of the Lord!
For what good is the day of the Lord to you?
It will be darkness, and not light.
It will be as though a man fled from a lion,
and a bear met him;
or as though he went into the house,
leaned his hand on the wall,
and a snake bit him.
Is not the day of the Lord darkness,
and not light?
Is it not very dark,
with no brightness in it?"
(Amos 5:18-20) (NKJV)

Since being forced off the air, Josh spent most of his time working at his computer communicating with the world outside via the internet. His favorite book was now the Holy Scripture on CD-ROM.

He screened all his phone calls, rarely returning them. His only confidant was Charlie, the doorman, who served as the middleman with the local grocer. His daily wardrobe had become a pair of sweats and a T-shirt. He couldn't remember how long it had been since he'd last had on a pair of shoes.

Being a hermit had suited him—giving him a chance to learn more about the God of his fathers.

A knock at the door interrupted the update of his Chit-chat page.

That's strange, he thought. *Where's Charlie?*

He looked through the peep hole and saw three men in dark suits. "What do you want?" he yelled through the door.

"Josh Cohen?"

"Yes." Josh didn't go into isolation to just open the door to anyone.

"SSS. We need to talk to you."

"Call my attorney," Josh yelled back. "I'm not giving interviews today." He chuckled to himself. "We have a court order," the man shouted back.

"I don't care what you have, I'm not opening this door. This is still America, isn't it?"

Josh watched through the peep hole as the men conferred among themselves and then reluctantly left. *Well,* he thought, *I guess it has started.*

He picked up the telephone and dialed the private international number.

"Ben Sadle here."

"Ben, this is Josh."

"Josh, good to hear from you. I was thinking about you yesterday. How's your situation?"

Josh could hear the excitement in Ben's voice.

"I think it's time to leave, Ben. I had three visitors from the SSS knocking on my door a while ago. Somehow they got through Charlie, my doorman. No one has ever gotten through Charlie before."

"How much time do you have?"

"Ben... I don't think I have any time to spare."

"Be careful, Josh."

"I will. See ya soon."

Josh went through his modest apartment packing the necessary clothing and legal papers, plus a few favorite photos. He was somewhat sentimental about leaving this apartment. He'd been very comfortable here these last six years. It wasn't fancy, but it met his needs and had been a nice place to get away from the demands of a hectic media career.

He looked around the room and thought about the books he'd written, the hours of listening to Mannheim Steamroller, the news, talk show programs and endless sports games he watched on TV, the numerous magazines and books he'd read.

He took a sip of diet coke. *This apartment has been a late-night haven for the best years of my life*, he thought.

"Father God," he said out loud, "Guide my steps and lead my path. I'm about to go out into the great unknown. Don't let me get lost."

He slipped down the backstairs and quickly let himself out with a key Charlie had given him several years ago. After his radio program had skyrocketed to the top, he was constantly pursued by the media or well-meaning fans. Good ole Charlie had come up with the idea that Josh could come and go at will through the janitor's entrance.

The sound of his hurried steps echoed off the dirty red brick walls that framed the alley. His tall frame splashed through the puddles that zigzagged down the alley two blocks to the corner. Stepping out into the busy New York traffic, he flagged a taxi and jumped in out of breath.

"Israeli Consulate, please."

I can't believe I'm running from my own country, he thought. *I never imagined I'd be seeking what amounts to asylum from Israel, the last bastion of a moral democracy.*

Tommy leaned over the stove, the steam from the large pot of vegetable stew enveloping his face. He stirred the mixture and put the lid down. He couldn't help but think it wouldn't be long until he'd be unable to get enough food to serve the last few of his faithful customers and friends—much less the food ministry he'd recently gotten involved with.

Food rationing after the rapture had caused runs on the grocery stores as well as runs on the banks, but the last year had stabilized food supplies. He knew this wouldn't last much longer.

The restaurant had been Tommy's life after his wife had left him for a college professor who used to come in and always ask for her section. It had taken the Lord to touch his broken heart and heal the hurt.

He thought back to that first Tuesday after the global earthquakes. He'd been surprised at the lone patron who stopped in for lunch. Tommy hadn't expected any customers that day due to the turmoil everywhere, but there he was fixing a club sandwich on wheat for his only customer. He could still hear the rich sound of his customer's voice as they discussed all the news.

Tommy was one of the first "Josh Room" restaurants, a place where people could go eat lunch and still listen to Josh's radio program. He hadn't paid much notice, until he heard the customer let out several hearty laughs.

"Do you listen to Josh Cohen often?" he asked, surprised that this man would so easily laugh at the pain the callers seemed to be enduring.

"Yes. I've listened to Josh for many, many years now," the man said.

"Oh, you must be from California then?" Tommy hadn't ever met anyone who had listened to Josh in his early years as a regular D.J.

"We go back further than that." The stranger smiled.

"So," Tommy asked confused, "what's so funny about Josh calling his friend Dave Malone in order to end all the speculation about some strange supernatural event, like that woman Sarah claimed?"

The man looked at Tommy with a gleam in his eyes. "Josh won't find his friend Dave Malone."

"How do you know?" Tommy propped his hands up on his hips, staining his white apron, as he challenged his only customer.

He remembered as if it were yesterday that man's explanation of the disappearances—how God had in the blink of an eye removed His children from the earth—and the plan he had for His Jewish remnant.

Tommy had wrestled with the truth for days after that, finally accepting the full truth of the Gospel. He had looked forward to sharing his conversion with that lone customer, never stopping to wonder how that man knew so much. But the stranger never come back.

Forming a Bible study group after that had been one of the most rewarding things in Tommy's life. And now, his food ministry to those too ill to provide for themselves kept in perspective how blessed he'd been with good health.

His thoughts came back to Harry's joking one night about the Bible study group moving to his mountain retreat in Colorado.

Maybe we ought to give it some serious consideration; he thought. *There wasn't anything keeping them in Austin. Nothing was permanent anymore.* He never dreamed he'd see himself in a position like what he'd endured lately.

He had spent his life working hard to build his business, regretting having placed all his faith in himself. Recent events confirmed how little control he actually had over his own life.

A knock at the back door interrupted his thoughts. Kevin and Donna sauntered in, Bibles in tow, dressed as usual in blue jeans and T-shirt.

"How's school going?" Tommy asked as he took their coats.

"Not good, Tommy," Donna said. "My poli-sci professor is real big on a oneworld system. Matter of fact, one of his hero's is Mikhail Gorbachev. Mr. Davis loves to quote to the class from Gorbachev's book *Perestroika*. His lecture today was all about how there are three causes of war—political conflicts, religious conflicts, and economic conflicts. He says that if we had a oneworld government, oneworld religion, and oneworld economy, we'd have a world of peace and security without conflicts."

"Wow," Tommy said, "I know the Bible foretells of a oneworld system, but it's something else to hear people talk about it and to see it happening in our lives. Have either of you ever read *Perestroika*?" Tommy asked.

They both shook their heads no.

"It's very interesting to note," he explained, "that Gorbachev believes that in order to achieve peace and security on earth we must stamp out religious conflict. His way of doing this would be to outlaw any religious exclusiveness and to make talking against another's religion a 'hate crime.' Obviously Satan realized communism couldn't keep man from God, so he's arranging it so that if you're going to allow religion into a political system you have to accept everyone's religion. To say that Jesus Christ is the only way would be in essence a 'hate crime' against another's beliefs."

The ring of the front bell sent an apprehensive chill through Tommy. "Most everyone lately uses the back door," he said. "I'll be right back." He wiped his hands off on the white apron he wore and disappeared down the long dark hall.

Kevin followed behind Tommy, his blood racing.

They reached the front door of the old cafe. "Who is it?" he shouted through the blacked-out glass door.

"SSS. Open up."

Kevin ran back to the kitchen and grabbed his backpack. "Get your stuff."

"What's wrong?" Donna asked, reaching for her coat.

"No time to talk about it. Just get your things. We've got to get out." Kevin rushed Donna through the back door. As they got in the car, Harry and Marilyn pulled in the back lot. Kevin swerved the car around, sending the gravel flying.

"Take off, guys. The SSS is at the front. It'll be bad for Tommy if they find us here."

Kevin followed Harry out of the parking lot.

"Kevin!" Donna clutched his arm as they reached the stop sign. "What about the others?"

"You're right," he said. The four tires squealed as Kevin whirled the car back around. Slowly he drove back and parked across the street, hoping to waylay anyone else arriving for Bible study. While they waited, Donna observed the eerie shadows on the hood of the car, created by the moon as the trees swayed back and forth overhead.

Kevin surveyed the back of the cafe. Downstairs was the kitchen and dining room. Tommy had turned the upstairs into living quarters a year or so ago, no longer able to afford the taxes on a house and business property.

Kevin and Donna watched as lights inside the building flicked on and then off. Each sat in silent prayer, asking God for Tommy's safety and a late arrival for the rest of their friends.

What seemed like hours later, the SSS pulled out of the parking lot. Kevin and Donna ducked to avoid being seen. Once the taillights blended into the early evening hues, they jumped out and ran across the street. Kevin pounded on the back door, "Tommy... it's me," he yelled. The bolt slid back and Tommy slowly opened the door. "Are you all right?" Kevin asked as he stepped inside. He stopped suddenly at the sight of Tommy's bloodied nose and cut eye. "What happened?" he cried.

"They gave me a warning," Tommy said, moving toward the sink for a wet rag.

"A warning about what?" Donna asked, clinging to Kevin. "They said they'd been informed that I was entertaining a 'hate group,' and they'd be keeping an eye on me."

Donna gasped.

"You were smart to get out. Thanks for thinking so fast. Saved my skin," Tommy said as he doctored his face.

"Doesn't look like we did you much good," Kevin joked, "but we did warn Harry and Marilyn."

"I wonder why no one else has shown up for Bible study?" Donna asked. "I hope the others haven't suffered the same visit."

Janet tossed and turned in her sleep. The big expensively covered fluffy white pillows fell to the floor. She kicked her white comforter to the foot of the bed. The cat jumped off the bed in search of a quiet place to sleep.

Janet dreamed of the three SSS men ripping carpet out, cutting her seats, and destroying her car in their search for some clue as to where she had hidden the Book.

"I didn't do anything," she screamed in her dream as one man grabbed her, violently shaking her arm.

"What have you done with the book?" he yelled.

"I don't know what book you're talking about." She sobbed and dropped to her knees. As she prepared to die from the gun aimed at her head, she heard a loud shout and running footsteps.

"Stop... I have papers from the Alzafar Grand Master. She's innocent. She doesn't have anything to do with those people."

Janet looked up through a haze of tears and saw John running toward them. "You've made a mistake. Don't hurt her," he demanded. He picked her up and cuddled her head against his chest.

"Why, why, why?" she wept.

She woke up moaning and writhing in her bed. An eerie feeling of being watched caused her skin to crawl.

What a horrible dream, she thought, reaching for her robe, now lying crumpled on the floor. She hurriedly turned on the light to chase away any fear lingering in the darkness. She put on her slippers and walked downstairs to the kitchen. Methodically, she removed the powdered cocoa from the cabinet and filled her cup with boiling water. She moved to the table and slumped down, staring at the picture of her mom and dad hanging on the wall by the telephone. Her Siamese cat jumped in her lap.

"Belvidere, what's happened to my life? What's happened to the whole world?" Tears rolled down her pale cheeks as she stroked the cat. Grief and the months of what had been controlled fear consumed her.

Why were those men at my car this afternoon? Why wouldn't John give me an explanation about that card? Why did I dream about some book?

Janet began to panic and reached for the telephone.

I've got to call someone. But I don't have any friends, except from Tommy's group.

Jealousy ate at her as she pictured Sally's unruly red curls and big brown laughing eyes. She lightly brushed her slender fingers across her lips.

No lipstick. I'm sitting here on the verge of panic and hearing my mother tell me to put on my lipstick. Sally doesn't need lipstick.

Janet swallowed her jealousy and dialed Sally's phone number.

"Sally," Janet softly breathed into the mouth piece.

"Janet, Janet, is that you?" Sally asked, trying to wake up.

"I'm really sorry to call you so late," Janet apologized, "but I need help."

"What's wrong? You're not hurt are you?"

"No, it's nothing like that. I just need to talk to someone. Bad dreams. Ah, I mean, I...I think I'm losing my mind." Janet gripped the phone with both hands.

"Don't panic," Sally ordered, "I'll be there in a few minutes."

Janet hung up the phone, sat down, and leaned her head on the table.

The word had passed around that Tommy's was no longer a safe place to meet for Bible study, so the group moved to Harry's apartment. They were all surprised to see Sally and Janet come in together. It had been several weeks since Janet had come around. Usually when someone got lax in attendance, they seldom returned to the fold.

"Hey, Janet," Stan said, "it's good to see you." He smiled, revealing straight white teeth.

"Yeah," chimed in Donna, "we've been missing you."

"Thanks," Janet said, her head downcast, ashamed at the things she'd been thinking about all of them.

Everyone gathered in Harry's apartment-sized living room. Donna and Kevin sat on one side of the couch and Marilyn at the other, with Stan in the recliner. Harry got two chairs from the kitchen for Sally and Janet and squatted down on the floor beside Tommy. "So tell us what's been happening in your life, Janet," Tommy said.

"I feel really bad," Janet began. "I've been bitter and angry and didn't want to see any of you again. You all have such a peace about what's happened to you and what we have to live through, again, with another Hitler."

Janet sniffled as she went on. "Then I met this guy in the capitol cafeteria, and I thought all my problems were solved. He seemed to really care about me and want to be with me. Things were going great until yesterday when I left work. There were three men with the SSS waiting for me at my car."

"You're kidding," Donna gasped, clutching Kevin's arm.

"Oh dear!" Marilyn said.

"I guess none of us will be spared," added Harry.

"So anyway," she continued, "they had a court order to search my car for 'hate crime' material. I couldn't believe it."

"What did you do?" Marilyn asked.

"I didn't do anything. John, the guy I'm...was dating pulled out some kind of card. The officer read it and gave it back, saying they'd made a mistake, and left."

"What kind of card was it?" Tommy frowned.

"When I asked John about it, he said he wanted to get out of there. He said he'd explain it to me later, but he never did."

"What happened after that?" Stan asked.

Janet began to cry. Sally leaned over and put her arm around her.

"Janet had a horrible nightmare last night and called me. I went over and we talked and read the Bible, and Janet accepted Jesus as her Messiah."

"Janet, that's wonderful," Kevin shouted and leaned over to give her a hug.

"Thanks." Janet smiled, wiping her eyes. "I feel bad about the way I've acted toward all of you. I hope you'll forgive me."

"Janet," Tommy said, "don't worry about us. We're glad that God opened your eyes and brought you back."

"Now," Tommy said as he rose from the floor, "we need to start thinking about what we're going to do when things get really bad. If you've noticed lately, the grocery stores aren't stocked like they were even six months ago. It's been hard enough to get just the basics."

Marilyn chimed in, "I had to go to three different stores the other day to get everything on my list, and it was a short list at that."

"What about you, Stan. How's life as a policeman these days?"

"It's pretty scary," Stan said.

"Like how?" Sally asked, alarmed.

"The people we're arresting these days are being arrested for heinous crimes. In past years we made arrests for public intoxication or petty theft, drug use and sales, and occasionally we'd catch a convenience store robber. Once in a while we'd even catch a drive-by shooter. But the kind of criminals we've been catching these last several months is scary. Even though lots of people weren't Christians, many people still had some sense of moral responsibility. Now we've got an overabundance of sickos—psychopathic murders, mutilators, perverts like you've never seen.

"It's bad. And the strange thing about it... we're catching them. They're making no effort to hide their crimes or hide from the law. Criminals these days are no respecter of age, race, or gender.

"They don't care who they kill or maim. These criminals have no remorse, no guilt. They're evil to the core, and even I'm starting to get scared."

The group was surprised to hear a statement like that coming from Stan. Stan looked like a world champion body builder and fully capable of taking care of himself.

"I'll tell you something else that scares me." Stan looked around at each one of them. "There is a pattern forming that appears to support the notion that the criminals have singled out victims who are either Christian or Jewish."

"Oh, my," Marilyn said, "what can we do to protect ourselves?"

"There's not anything you can do, short of never leaving your house," Stan said. "And even that's no guarantee. "The Holy Scriptures say God's judgment will include ecological damage, economic disaster, rampant crime, persecution, a one-world government and a one-world religion, famines, plagues, death, destruction, and wars such as never have been fought."

"But," Janet spoke up, "it hasn't been that bad here."

"You're right. We've been somewhat insulated, living here in Texas. But I'm afraid as the food situation worsens we'll be in constant danger.

"Y'all know about Harry's place in the Colorado mountains. We've talked about it. And as much as neither of us wants to leave our homes and businesses, we both feel in order to adequately feed and protect ourselves, we need to be somewhere we can grow our own food and be away from the big cities.

"What about beasts that no longer having a fear of man that it talks about in Revelation? Won't we be in danger somewhere out in the wilderness?" Sally asked.

"Think about it for a moment, Sally," Harry said. "When people are going hungry, the last thing they're going to do is to feed their pets. Eventually there will be wild cats and dogs in the streets looking for food. There's going to be large rodents, insects, birds. And more than likely they'll congregate in the cities where they've found food in the past."

The girls did a collective shiver.

"And we need to think about the mark of the beast. No one without that mark will be able to buy or sell." Tommy surveyed the faces of the people around him and then continued, "I feel our ministry will be helping people survive the coming holocaust, and I'd feel better knowing we had a place prepared once evil breaks loose."

Tommy let his eyes roam over the group. "And," he hesitated, "we've got to be prepared to die for our faith. In Revelation 6:9, after the fifth seal is broken, the souls of those slain because of the Word of God and the testimony they maintained are seen under the altar in heaven."

The room grew deathly silent. "Dear God, Most Holy Father," Tommy began, "we entrust our lives into your hands. We know your judgment is coming upon the earth. We beseech you to use our lives to glorify your name. In the name of the Messiah. Amen."

"Tommy, when do you think we need to leave? Don't we have a year or so to get ready for the worst?" Sally asked, tears in her eyes.

"Yes, I think you're probably right. But it'll take one season just to grow enough food to meet our immediate needs. Obviously we can't do anything right now in the dead of winter, but as spring begins we should be in place to make the most of the time available. I would suggest we start buying nonhybrid seeds and nonperishable food staples. Above all, we should make ourselves as inconspicuous as possible. The last thing we want to do is to alert the SSS of our intentions.

"But before we leave tonight, I have a special prayer request." Tommy looked around the coffee table. "You all know that I'm involved in a ministry to deliver meals to those too ill to provide for themselves—mostly Aids patients. But recently my delivery list has grown to include people suffering from pain so bad that nothing eases it. Doctor's don't know what causes it. Some are saying it's a mutant virus not susceptible to antibiotics, and others think it's a result of chemical warfare. Whatever it is it's bad. Please keep me in your prayers as I minister to these people about Jesus."

The pain, the excruciating pain.

He screamed for his nurse.

What a sorry excuse of humanity. Why did the agency send me the ugliest, fattest and cruelest woman on the earth. I deserve better than this!

He grimaced.

I think she's shooting me full of diet coke.

He cursed, another surge of pain racing through his body. *Surely there's something stronger in a society as advanced as ours to kill pain.*

"Nurse," he screamed again. "Where is that witch?" he mumbled between clinched teeth.

She's probably sleeping off a large lunch.

Suffering the endless pain and exhaustion he slid off the bed.

I'm ending this nightmare now!

His resolve drove him to the floor. He grimaced from the effort, but the thought of blood soaking his linens seemed almost as obscene as the obese nurse the government forced him to live with.

If only she could feel my pain.

He tried to laugh but the grin turned into a groan.

She'll soon understand my pain. She'll regret the day she ever laid eyes on me.

The bathroom seemed miles away from the foot of his bed. The pain he endured would break the sanity of most men, he was sure. The only thing propelling him to the bathroom on his belly like a snake was the delight in knowing the nurse from hell would suffer more than he.

Surely hours had passed by the time he reached up to shut the bathroom door after dragging his legs across the threshold.

He laid his face down on the cold gray tile until the heaving motion of his chest subsided. He lay as still as possible. Even the fibers of the bath mat caused pain to shoot through his fingers and up his arms.

That stupid nurse! I could be dead by now and she wouldn't even know it. She probably won't find me till that Jew boy cook brings my dinner.

His hatred of the woman, licensed by the government as his caretaker, and Jews in general, gave him the strength necessary to pull himself up onto the pedestal sink. He opened the medicine chest and reach for the razorblades placed neatly beside his razor and shaving cream.

He was almost tempted to go through the cabinet and toss all the medicines and personal items he wouldn't be needing. The pain stopped him.

He groaned, gently sliding into the tub. He sat up and turned the round porcelain knobs labeled H and C. He turned the knob boldly displaying the H as far as it would go.

The sound of water gushing from the spout brought a moment's peace. He closed his eyes and savored the warm water that began to cradle his thin body. The water got hotter and inched up his belly. Steam rose and fogged the mirror.

He forced himself to open his eyes. The pain brought an end to the soothing effects of the hot water. He took the razor blade in one hand and raised the other. He studied his bony wrist and bulging veins. Methodically, he placed the tip into his skin and slowly dragged the blade down. Blood spurt forth and raced down toward his elbow.

The steaming water crawled up his body, tickling his chest hairs. He forced his eyes away from staring at the blood that covered his hand. He reached forward to shut off the faucet.

The water turned dark red as blood from his other wrist squirted into the tub. He marveled at the pulsating flow of both wrists until he grew lightheaded. He closed his eyes and let the tub cradle his neck.

The late afternoon sun cast a dull hue through the thin dirty curtain that covered the small window. The bath water grew cold. Time slipped away.

Outside the house, Tommy pulled up to the curb in his Park Avenue. The front lawn was overgrown and Ivy had begun to violate the shuttered windows.

The front door was answered by the UniversalCARE In-Home Companion. She greeted Tommy with the usual grunt and lead him to the bedroom. She stifled the urge to hold her nose as she pushed open the door. It took a minute for her eyes to adjust to the darkness.

"Mr. Peterson." She didn't care if she woke him up. "Mr. Peterson," she said louder. "Your dinner is here."

She was surprised to find the bed empty. "That's odd. He's barely been able to use the bedpan these last couple of months."

She turned to the bathroom. "Mr. Peterson? Mr. Peterson?"

She hesitated, then turned to Tommy, "If I see that old coot on the pot I'll loose my appetite for sure!"

She pushed the door open, then jerked backward into Tommy. She screamed, turning to bury her face on Tommy, who had a hard time containing his own emotion.

At the sound of the scream, hollow eyes popped open and a skinny body lunged forward in the tub. A curse escaped Peterson's lips. "Oh shut up, you stupid woman!"

She turned around at his words and grabbed her heart. His meanness enraged her. An evilness swelled in her breast. "Curse God and die you horrible old man."

He leaned back and closed his eyes. His arms were limp. "I'm trying to die. Oh, how I'm trying. Why does death elude me?"

The grocery store was crowded. Gas prices were astronomical, shipping was slow, and fewer items were stocked on the shelves. What was available to shoppers was bought up quickly. Janet had to shop daily to get even the basics.

She hated grocery shopping, but managed to hum a song as she looked for the shortest check-out line. She felt, for the first time, a real peace in her life. The renewed fellowship with Sally and the others strengthened her hope for tomorrow.

"Janet... hi," said a voice behind her.

"Oh, John, hi," she stuttered, startled to see him.

He moved his basket to block her.

"I'm getting the feeling you've been avoiding me lately."

"No, I've just been busy." She pushed her cart around him to another checkout line.

"Too busy to even return my calls?" He caught up with her. "I've looked for you at the capitol cafeteria. I came by your office yesterday, but the secretary said you were out."

"Sorry, I didn't get the message." Janet avoided his eyes.

"Have I done something wrong?" He put his hand on her basket.

"No, I've just been busy, that's all," she said, reaching over to get a magazine.

John stared into her shopping cart. "Why all this dried food stuff? Beans, rice, packaged soups, bottled water. Looks like you're planning for some kind of disaster. What's the deal, Janet? It's against the law to stockpile food."

People started to stare at them.

"I'm not, John. I know the law. Remember I'm a lawyer." She rolled her eyes. "This is just how I eat." She buried her head in the magazine.

"Sorry, don't get offended. If I didn't know better, I'd think you'd been hanging out with your 'end of the world' friends again."

She turned the pages and ignored him.

"Oh no, come on. Don't tell me you're listening to them again." He helped her unload her basket onto the conveyer belt. "Don't you know they'll just get you in trouble."

Janet's face turned red as she realized people were studying her. She paid for her items and left without turning back to look at John.

He paid for a pack of Trident and hurried out behind her.

"Janet, say something. Don't ignore me. I'm concerned about your safety. Can't you understand that those people you're hanging around with are bad news? Didn't that incident at your car show you anything?"

"It showed me that I can't trust you, John. Now please excuse me." She put the last sack in the front seat of her red 240ZX and shut the door. John stood there, his eyes pleading with her as she backed up.

By the time Janet pulled into her driveway, she was shaking. She jumped out of the car, leaving the groceries behind. She ran into the house, barely making it into the bathroom before throwing up the clear yellow bile that had formed in her stomach. Stumbling to the bedroom she lay down on her bed.

Lord, why am I so weak?

The loud shriek of the telephone brought her upright with a start. She hesitated before answering, "Hello."

"Janet, I've got to talk to you." Hearing John's voice, she let out a sob and slammed the phone down.

John hung the receiver up, confused about Janet's behavior. He wanted to warn her about the danger she was in, but at the same time he didn't want to make himself conspicuous by chasing after her. He'd been dressed down by the Worshipful Master at the last lodge gathering for flashing his card and foiling any investigation of a 'hate group member.'

John had begun to get a little irritated at all the talk of these hate groups. His lodge had recently been collecting membership rolls of churches and synagogues for the SSS. This secret collection of information had never bothered him in the past, but there was something different about it now. If he'd been a religious person, he'd be inclined to say there was something evil permeating the organization, especially since the earthquake when a large number of members, without explanation, stopped coming and quit paying dues.

Just forget it, he told himself, *don't get hung up on some goofy woman waiting for the end of the world.*

Josh was used to traveling by private plane. He had become too famous to travel comfortably as the rest of the world did. He was also used to the luxury of wealth that allowed such privileged travel, but being in the prime minister's plane brought with it the awe afforded someone of that stature.

He pushed nagging thoughts of the future from his mind and reclined in the large comfortable chair. The dull roar of the jet engine faded in the background as he closed his eyes. Thoughts of the last couple of hours invaded his head.

He had used the phone from the Israeli consulate and said his good-byes to his friends, offering jobs to his old staff. None were anxious to head over to the war-torn region of the Middle East. Most of his friends would have thought he was nuts had they not understood the danger he was in of being imprisoned for treason. Josh contemplated the call he'd made to his attorney. The SSS had been busy after they left his apartment. "Josh, what did you do to make those guys so mad?"

"I didn't do beans. They came banging on my door unannounced and I just wouldn't open it. Told them I wasn't giving interviews today."

"I swear, Josh. Can't you learn to stay out of trouble?"

"Oh, lighten up, Scott. It's not that bad. I'm getting a free trip to Israel. I'll be in the very middle of things during the final days, and I'll have my show back and be broadcasting worldwide. What could be better?"

"Josh, I've been concerned about you lately, buddy. What do you mean 'the final days'?"

Collecting his thoughts and praying he could explain something so new to himself, he said, "We're living in the final years of life as we know it on earth. Jesus called the Christians to heaven, and those of us remaining have to endure the coming wrath on those who refuse to acknowledge Jesus as Lord."

"You're starting to sound like my neighbor, Josh."

"So where is your neighbor?" Josh twisted the phone cord.

"I don't know, I haven't seen him in a while. I'm not his keeper. He must be on a business trip or something."

"Where's his family?" Josh asked.

"Come to think of it, I haven't seen them lately either, but..."

"Don't take my word for it, Scott. Go find a Christian bookstore if that's still possible, or else borrow a Bible from someone and read it for yourself in the book of Revelation. But I'm telling you we're in Jacob's Seventieth Week, and those who don't call upon the Lord will suffer in eternity."

"You're starting to make me nervous."

"Whatever it takes, friend."

"Take care of yourself, Josh."

"You too, Scott." Josh closed his eyes and prayed, "Lord, show him the way like you showed me."

It was early morning when the cabin attendant woke him. "Mr. Cohen, we're in Jerusalem."

He woke with a start, forgetting where he was and all that had happened in the previous months. He sat for a moment, then his memory came rushing back like a lead ball knocking him into a foggy reality. Ben was at the gate to welcome him. They embraced as Josh got off the plane.

"My friend, it is good to see you."

"Thanks, Ben, it's good to be here. You're a lifesaver."

"Not at all, Josh. You're doing me a favor." As they drew apart, Josh was distracted by the beautiful dark-haired woman standing in Ben's shadow. Ben noticed he had lost Josh's attention. "Oh," he said, stepping back, "I'd like to introduce you to my assistant and oldest daughter Ariel."

"It's nice to make your acquaintance." She offered her hand.

"The pleasure is all mine," Josh said, captured by her deep blue eyes.

Ben smiled to himself. He'd never known a man not to be captured by Ariel's beauty. It pleased him that Josh was no different.

"Josh, if you don't mind, I've asked Ariel to assist you in finding acceptable living quarters. Several pressing matters await my attention at the office, and I must get back. I've made dinner reservations for us at eight this evening and will send a car around for you."

"No problem, Ben. I'll see you then."

Ariel showed Josh the two best housing units in the city. After he made his selection, she handled all the negotiations and lease arrangements in Hebrew. She coordinated the delivery of his meager possessions and then insisted on taking him to lunch while his apartment was being readied.

"I don't think I've ever seen anyone work quite like you do," Josh said as they waited to be served.

"Dad taught his children the value of speed and efficiency as we were growing up, and it has paid off well in these turbulent times."

"How many kids are in your family?" he asked.

"There are five of us now. Three girls and two boys, we lost one brother in the recent war."

"I'm sorry." Josh wondered why Ben hadn't told him.

"It's all right. He died a hero fighting for the holy city."

Josh was eager to change the subject, "So, how about you? Husband? Kids?"

"I've never married," she answered and for the first time avoided his eyes.

Josh suddenly got very excited about the future.

When he crawled into bed that night, he had little time to think about the events of the day before exhaustion consumed him and pulled him into a deep sleep.

Ariel went to sleep with a smile on her face for the first time in several years. Her father lay awake into the early hours of the morning, gripped by an unfathomable, suffocating fear.

The next morning, Josh felt refreshed, bursting with a renewed sense of purpose. Ariel pulled up at nine in her bronze Honda Accord. They drove through the narrow streets of western Jerusalem to his new office, a studio located in an old three-story building close to the Knesset.

Josh was shocked to see armed soldiers in the foyer as they entered. "What's in this building?"

Ariel shrugged. "Just a few organizations. The Israeli office of the ADL, our team of peace negotiators, the Vatican embassy, and the new Palestinian embassy."

"Oh, that's comforting," he laughed.

Ariel had hired the necessary staff, subject to Josh's approval. The studio shined with state-of-the-art equipment and the most magnificent, golden, B-16 microphone. Josh was flabbergasted. He had been respected in New York, but never catered to quite like this.

"Let me introduce you to Eli Meyer, your call screener," Ariel said as she took Josh's arm. "He is fluent in nine languages, Hebrew, Arabic, Farsi, Turkish, Russian, Sudanese, English, German and French, in addition to having some knowledge of Japanese and Italian."

"Wow, that's great! But how will I understand the caller?" Josh questioned.

"There is an automatic translation device built into the system. Not only will you be able to understand the caller, but the show will be broadcast in the spoken language of each country receiving the signal as it is beamed in from the satellite."

"You are kidding," he said in amazement. "I'll be broadcasting worldwide and in every language?"

"That's right." She smiled, seeing Josh's childlike excitement.

"I can't believe it. This is every talk show host's dream. Thank you, Lord," he shouted as he twirled around in his new chair.

Ariel was caught off guard hearing him give thanks to a higher being. "When do you want to premier the show?" she asked.

"Today. Why wait? Looks like you've got everything set up. Do you think this part of the world is ready for me?"

"We'll know before long," she said. "I think we have your theme music ready. What time do you want to start the show?"

"The majority of my previous audience will be asleep. What do you suggest?"

"You can continue to start the show as usual at eleven a.m., and we can set a time delay so that the signal is broadcast to North America at eleven standard time the next day."

"Perfect." He clapped his hands together. "Ariel, you're great!"

She smiled at him, grateful for the appreciation. Men in Israel seldom offered it.

Josh grew unusually nervous, sitting in his new studio with all its new equipment. His staff in New York was a mixture of colors and genders, but the dominant middle-eastern characteristics and dress of his new staff would take some getting used to.

He gripped the Jerusalem Post headlines. Beads of sweat popped out on his forehead. *This is ridiculous*, he thought to himself. *I've been doing this for years. Why am I so nervous?*

"Lord," he silently prayed, "I'm assuming you've got me where you want me. I'm leaving this up to you to accomplish your will."

Thadd, the show's producer, started the countdown as the theme music blared in the background. Josh watched as Thadd's fingers indicated the time to air, one, two, three. The green "on the air" light flashed brightly, and Josh jumped in without missing a beat.

"Shalom, friends and fellow chatters, across what has become the fruity plain. It's me, I'm back, sitting at my real radio announcer's desk. That's right, folks. Your old friend, or new friend, whichever the case may be, Josh Cohen. Coming to you live from Jerusalem, the new home of the Democracy In Action Network. The giant of talk radio, blasting at you with 29.842 megahertz on the shortwave. A screaming mimi of information exploding into every country and in every language. Don't go away, we'll be back with more."

Ariel grinned from ear to ear. "Father said you were great, but I could never quite imagine what a radio talk show would be like."

"Just hang around. You ain't seen nothin' yet." Josh flashed her a big smile as the green on-light blazed again.

"I'm here, folks, and as long as I'm here, it doesn't really matter where here is. Now, for those of you hearing me for the first time, let me warn you that I don't pull any punches. You may ask why I've left the United States. To be honest, it wasn't something I wanted to do. But the United States can no longer be called the land of the free. Democracy has been tossed out with the bath water, and the country has been covered with a blanket of oppression called Executive Order 12148." Josh paused in his monologue to let Thadd play the funeral march.

"That's the United State's new national anthem," Josh laughed. "Now, I realize all this may be news to those of you on this side of the Atlantic, and you may be wondering what Executive Order 12148 is. You thought things were status quo with Emily running the presidency until husband Bob could be found. Folks, I'm here to tell you that President Bob Wells will never return to the presidency, and Emily knows that and has taken control."

Josh pounded the table.

"She has seized control of the country. She has suspended both the House of Representatives and the Senate, and it's going to get worse. I'm telling you the truth.

"Emily and her partners in crime have created a new agency called the SSS, a department comparable to the KGB. Folks, if you thought the KGB was bad, it can't even hold a candle to the SSS."

Josh rapped the table with his thumb. "Let me tell you Emily's other plans. She's going to censor all media and remove your right of free speech." Josh stopped to listen to Thadd. "You say she can't do that? Well, she's doing it. She did it to me. Ha, so she thought," Josh joked.

"But putting me aside, she has taken control of all sources of power: petroleum, gas, electrical, and nuclear. She's ordered a ten p.m. curfew nationwide, enforced by the SSS, I might add. She's now controlling all health, welfare, and education. She's even controlling the little general himself, Ford Devoe. Ha! I never thought that possible." Josh snickered.

"Folks, seriously, I'm saying she has nationalized the whole United States. And," he paused for emphasis, "so as not to cause an all-out revolt by raising taxes again, she has removed the tax exemption on churches to create tax money that she says rightfully belongs to the people and which will more than adequately pay for the necessary employees to take over the public business sector. All churches, that is, except the 'The World Church of Everlasting Peace,' which she claims is the official church of the White House and therefore tax exempt as part of the government. Can you believe that?" he cried.

"All this in a country that rose up from a group of people, uniting together out of a desire to freely worship. A people who, once again, are being forced to submit to the bondage of the quote official religion end of quote."

Josh shuffled some papers. "I'm sorry, people. I just can't believe she is getting away with it." He shook his head. "In addition to this — I know you can't believe there's more — but Emily has put into operation her new information super highway, a system of collecting personal information on every individual. A bill that had been pigeonholed in House committee last year will now eliminate all privacy once you make use of any government program, law enforcement included.

"My friends, you so much as get stopped for a traffic violation and they've 'gotch ya.' Let's take a break and we'll be right back."

"You're listening to the Democracy In Action Network, a program of Jerusalem Free Radio," the announcer said after the commercial break. "Stay tuned for the last hour, coming next."

"I'm back, Josh Cohen in dogged pursuit of the truth. Now back to Emily. She has outlawed the possession of firearms except by the SSS. And, believe it or not, she has empowered the attorney general's office to prosecute 'hate groups' to the full extent of the law. The full extent being whatever punishment the Judge deems necessary to end any particular behavior."

The studio staff began winding down the callers. Josh didn't want anyone left hanging on when time in the last hour expired.

Thadd looked over at Ariel. It was hard not to see how she admired the American.

"So what do you think of our newest sensation, Ariel?" Thadd grinned.

"Oh, I don't know." Ariel blushed at his question. She quickly turned away to avoid further discussion. She looked through the glass and watched Josh interact with his listeners through a large microphone hanging in the air. She couldn't decide what it was about him that appealed to her. He was tall and kind of average looking, but there was just something about him that made you want to give him a big hug.

"Oops, I'm out of time, folks. Sorry we didn't get to more of your calls today, but with a brand-new audience I felt it was necessary to bring everyone up to speed. Same time, same place tomorrow. See ya."

The studio erupted in applause as they went off the air. The three hours had passed with no hitches.

"I guess I had weeks of pentup monologue that there was no holding back." John grinned.

Everyone laughed. Josh noticed a light in Ariel's eyes, and his heart began to race.

Across the ocean, Harry regularly listened to the "underground" news programs on his shortwave radio. As he fiddled with a particular computer program designed to compute food volume input vs. output, he was astounded to hear the theme song for Josh Cohen.

Are they playing reruns? he wondered. He picked up the phone to call Tommy. Tommy assured him they wouldn't be playing reruns and quickly hung up to go find his short wave radio.

Headlines the next morning confirmed they hadn't been listening to reruns. "Cohen Reappears as Radio's Giant Broadcasting WorldWide."

Most mornings at the White House were fairly quiet. Even from their first night, the First family had gotten into a habit of entertaining well into the early morning hours and sleeping until around noon. This necessitated cramming the wide array of the usual business meetings into a single afternoon. The staff stayed frazzled and tormented daily by lobbyists who claimed the president had no time for them now that he was president.

The idea that he didn't work normal business hours as did the rest of the country never occurred to them.

However, Emily now wanted to squeeze out every possible moment of power she could get. She sat at the breakfast table simmering in anger as she read the morning papers. "I can't believe he's back again. Get Joni Rains in here," she yelled at no one in particular, expecting whoever heard to obey. *I thought we locked him up*, she seethed. *I'm halfway tempted to cut all ties with Israel if they don't ban him from their airwaves.*

Joni strolled into the room. As attorney general she enjoyed immense power and had begun to resent Emily's constant, annoying summons.

"I thought I told you to get rid of that madman," Emily screeched at Joni, who stood there, smug in her tailored black wool Dior suit.

"I sent three of my top men to his apartment in New York to do just that. He wouldn't let them in." She shrugged.

"And?" Emily screamed.

"And they went to see his attorney? Josh is a popular man. We had to tread lightly. I didn't want to cause a riot. When they got back to his apartment, he was gone—nowhere to be found."

"His attorney, his attorney!" Emily wailed in disbelief. "I've placed the country under federal emergency management, and you send men to his attorney. His attorney has no rights! You let him slip right out from under you, and now he's broadcasting worldwide, in every language, and he's talking trash about me. I don't like it. I want him gone, finished, out of my hair forever. Do you understand?" Her screams could be heard throughout the executive wing.

Joni left Emily's office in a huff.

I am sick of that woman.

She stormed down the long hall oblivious to the empty stares from pictures of long since dead First Ladies hanging on the wall.

I know, she thought. *I'll call Ford Devoe. He's plenty mad at her himself. Besides hating Josh Cohen probably more than Emily does.*

For the first time since entering the White House that morning, a smile came to her face.

Joni could hardly contain herself before reaching the privacy of her office, and her secure phone line.

She punched the intercom button to her secretary.

"Martin, be a dear and hold all my calls."

"Yes, Ms. Rains."

She dialed the number Devoe had given her a few weeks earlier.

"Devoe here."

"Mr. Devoe, this is Joni Rains. Emily wants to move up the power blackout."

"Oh." Devoe coughed into the receiver.

Joni rolled her eyes as she held the receiver back from her ear.

Uncouth rich Texas trash!

Devoe continued, "Emily and I were just discussing that yesterday. She was adamant about waiting till the end of the month—something about the SSS not being ready to stage the riots."

"That's all been taken care of," Joni rushed in, angry that Emily had blamed her for the delay.

"Whatever." Devoe was tired of Emily and her excuses. "All I have to do is call the right people. They'll push a button here and a button there and it's lights out."

"So, Joni," he questioned. "Why are you calling instead of Ms. President?

Joni sat up straight in her chair. "She's busy—with Josh Cohen and all."

A menacing anger crept into Devoe's voice. "I'm working on that blackout next." He slammed the phone down.

Joni smiled as she gently laid the receiver in its cradle.

It was 7:00 p.m. Washington, D.C. time. A heavy fog blanketed the city. Streets were crowded with cars, casting an eerie glow into the night as people rushed to and fro about their lives.

Emily gently touched the white linen napkin to her lips and gazed across the small candlelit table at Tom. "Won't you be missed at the station tonight?"

He shook his head. "No, nothing big to report. I called in sick. I needed a day off anyway." He smiled at her. "Besides, what could be more important than an intimate dinner meeting with the president of the United States?"

Emily giggled. She scooted her chair back then suddenly the dimly lit wall chandeliers flashed off.

"What was that?" She stood up. The glow of candle light shimmered as she made her way to the door.

"You did pay your electric bill, didn't you?" Tom joked.

She tossed her head back and looked over her shoulder at him. "Don't be silly. I can assure you the electric company wouldn't shut off the White House."

Emily reached the door as the Secret Service burst into the room. A large beam of light blinded her. "Get that out of my face, you idiot!"

"Sorry, ma'am. Are you okay?"

"What is going on? Why are the lights off?"

Tom admired the back of Emily as she stood there in her purple dinner dress and high heels. Her feet were slightly apart and her hands were firmly placed on shapely hips.

"It's a total blackout, ma'am."

"A what!" Emily clinched her teeth and screamed, "Get me Joni Rains."

Israel denied demands for Josh's extradition to the U.S. for treason. Josh and Ben joked over the letter from the attorney general's office.

"That is one bodacious woman," Josh laughed.

"Yeah. I think you're safe over here, Josh. That is, if the hazards of mother nature don't get you. We've had some strange weather lately. I don't understand it."

"Ben, I hate to tell you this, but things are just going to get worse."

"Thanks a lot, friend. I was hoping you would bring us better luck." Ben smiled.

Josh raised his eyebrows, carefully thinking exactly how to say what he wanted to say. "No, I don't think I'm going to bring you luck. But maybe I can explain the whats and why of things soon to occur."

Ben didn't understand what Josh was getting at, which wasn't that unusual, but he did know that Emily Wells had no intentions of giving up until she had Josh's head on a platter.

"Get the pope on the phone," Emily hollered to her secretary after her call to the Israeli prime minister was refused for the third time. "Maybe he can use his influence with those stubborn Jews. What do they think is so great about Josh Cohen? Don't they know he's a greedy, hate-filled racist who should be punished for his crimes against the United States government?

"And get Joni Rains in here. This is all her fault. If she had done her job right the first time, I wouldn't be going through this. You'd think she could at least write a letter explaining to the prime minister exactly what is going to happen to Israel if they don't turn Josh Cohen over to American authorities." Emily threw her coffee cup across the room, regretting the absence of a target.

The pope's private offices glittered with a vulgar show of wealth. Simon insisted on the remodeling after convincing his staff that someone in his position must be surrounded by beautiful things.

"Your Eminence," Monsignor Lucci interrupted, "it's Emily Wells' office on the phone."

"Good grief! That woman's a pain," he moaned. "Can't she make a decision without calling me first? Okay, I'll take the call." The pope got comfortable, psyching himself up for the certain ordeal before him. "My dear Emily, how good to hear from you."

"Your Eminence, thank you for taking my call. I'll get right to the point. I know you're a busy man doing God's work."

Simon Peter thought to himself, *This must be serious. She's really sucking up.*

"I need your help regarding Israel." She instantly had his attention.

"Israel?" he questioned.

"That's right. They have allowed Josh Cohen to broadcast his talk show from Jerusalem, and they have refused our request of extradition for his blatant crimes of treason."

"Yeah, you're right. Seems like I heard his show recently." Simon struggled to contain his laughter. "As far as I know, Josh doesn't pose a threat to me or the church."

"Wha...doesn't pose a threat! Why…why that man is disclosing sensitive issues concerning our national security. He's probably over there giving the Israeli government top-secret information."

Emily began to shriek.

"Top secret, Emily?" Simon asked. "You mean like announcing to the world that you and your Secretary of Health and Human Services Diane Shannon use the same escort service?"

"That's a lie!" she yelled.

Simon grimaced at the volume of her voice. "Emily, Emily, calm down. Dear child, of course it was a lie. I see what you mean."

No wonder the inner circle has hinted at her elimination. I don't think I can take much more of her myself.

"I can help you, Emily, but in exchange you must also help me."

"Of course, anything," she quickly agreed.

"Making 'The World Church of Everlasting Peace' the official church of the U.S. was of great benefit to the stabilization of the world. But there is a growing faction, particularly in Texas, that is becoming quite bothersome to me."

"Even with our new anti-exclusion law that forbids any one religion from claiming theirs to be the only true faith?" she argued, surprised at his concern over a small group of dissenters.

"The anti-exclusion law is an excellent law," he agreed, "but it didn't go quite far enough. I need you to outlaw any religious gathering except in approved 'The World Church of Everlasting Peace' facilities."

"Done, but what about my problem?" she insisted.

"Don't worry about it, Emily. I'll see that it's taken care of," he said, growing weary of her shrieking voice.

Devoe hung up the phone and propped his alligator boots on his antique desk.

Emily did a sorry job of getting rid of that loud, boastful piece of scum. And now she's got Joni Rains mad at her. That lady is some piece of work. But I've got other more important matters to deal with right now.

The pieces were now all in place to establish Jerusalem as an International City. But with Josh Cohen over there stirring the world up about some story called Jacob's Seventieth Week, the inner circle was getting nervous.

Devoe studied the pattern in his boots.

We're going to have to speed up the process. We can't take all the time we planned in the beginning.

9

"And he causeth all,
both small and great,
rich and poor, free and bond,
to receive a mark in the right hand
or in their foreheads,
and that no man might buy or sell
save he that had the mark
or the name of the beast
or the number of his name."
(Revelation 13:16, 17)

Josh flinched as he read the international news report of the new currency distributed by the recently completed U.S. Mint in Houston, Texas. The new mint had been constructed, thanks to the generous donation of land by Ford Devoe.

Now it would no longer be necessary to exchange currency when traveling internationally. The value of the currency would be determined by its color, thus identifying the sponsoring country. Devoe had been a major player in the negotiating of the World Trade Treaty. With his private international airport in Houston now fully operational, he stood to gain more money and more power with the signing of WTT. Josh had never trusted Devoe, nor his so-called "selfless" motives. He had nearly exploded one day at lunch when Ben told him about the arrangement Israel had with DCI.

"Ben, that guy is a dictator looking for a home. You've got to get rid of him."

Ben set down his glass of wine. "I understand how you feel, Josh, but his office is the one that told us of the build-up of troops, thereby warning us of the attack."

"I'm sure that's true, but how long did they wait before they told you? Did you have adequate time to prepare for a major assault? Would you have been able to pull a victory off had God not intervened?" Josh pleaded with him to see the truth.

"Josh, I need to ask you something," Ben changed the subject.

"Sure, anything."

Ben took a deep breath. "I'm not supposed to be talking about the agreement." Ben lowered his voice and leaned into the table. "I think we've arrived at a tentative agreement, regarding Jerusalem and her protection, but I value your opinion and friendship."

"Okay, Ben. Spill it."

Ben hesitated, rubbing his hands together, wanting to stall the inevitable disapproval of his friend.

"As you know, since the war, and the virtual annihilation of the Muslim forces, the United Nations has been involved in working with us to arrive at another peace treaty agreeable to all parties.

"One of the big points," he continued, "is still the sovereignty of the Palestinians and their control of the borders of Jericho and Gaza. The UN has suggested we allow UN Command troops to patrol those borders.

"Of course," he said as if to reassure himself, "there will be both Israeli and Palestinian military participating in the UN forces. The PLO has agreed to this.

"The second objection, and probably the biggest, is the status of Jerusalem. The UN has agreed, along with the PLO and Muslim coalition, not to interfere with our decision to rebuild the Temple on the Temple Mount, one hundred feet south of the Dome of The Rock, if we will call Jerusalem an international city."

Ben paused, waiting for an outburst from Josh. When there was no response, he continued.

"As you know, we cling to the words of the prophets of Israel, as we stated in the Jerusalem Covenant, 'That all the inhabitants of the world shall enter within the gates of Jerusalem.' So we'll allow Jerusalem to be called an international city. However, the EC's new world president will have to sign the Jerusalem Covenant, thus showing his confirmation of our Covenant that Jerusalem, 'unified and whole, is the capitol of Israel'."

Josh, stone-faced, allowed Ben to finish explaining what Josh considered to be the final nail in the coffin of the sovereignty of Israel. He hesitated to say anything. Josh knew how much pressure Ben had been under, not only to be a strong prime minister since the death of Itzak Rabin, but because he was dedicated to doing the best for his country.

"Ben, you know we've always had differences of opinion on political issues. You're much further to the left than I've ever been. Maybe your heart is larger than mine. Maybe you see more good in people than I do." Josh shook his head. "You know you'll always have my full support, but I've got to tell you that I think you're making a grave mistake by allowing the United Nations to decide your future. Ben, mark my words, this peace won't last. And when it's broken, it'll be worse than before."

The following day, the plan went onto the fast track. Israel declared Jerusalem an international city, a city for all peoples and all religions. UN forces were quick to move in as peacekeepers and put an end to the daily gunfire heard in the old city.

The Vatican voiced its approval. The United Nations voted Ford Devoe in as Secretary General, and the Economic Community's inner circle hired as World President, Christopher Heinman, a newcomer to the world scene.

Heinman had been praised for his large financial support of the new Temple project, and many embraced him, a German Jew, as the eradication of Hitler's sin of Jewish annihilation.

Devoe insisted on keeping his offices in Houston even after being named UN secretary general. He had no desire to work out of some office in Brussels and listen to the mindless mutterings of people he couldn't understand.

After several rings, he answered his own phone. He cursed his new secretary.

Aren't there any qualified people left in the world?

"Devoe here," he said, trying to hide his exasperation. "Mr. Devoe, this is Christopher Heinman."

"Mr. President, how's it going?"

"Couldn't be better." Christopher laughed to himself. "I wanted to thank you for your influence with the Council on Foreign Relations and the EC. I know it had a great deal to do with my being hired as world president."

"My pleasure. I know you'll be a good president, and with Jerusalem now an international city, we felt it necessary to have a world president who had a financial interest in seeing real peace on earth. Will I see you at the Bilderberg meeting in Brussels to discuss and formulate the new world agenda?"

"Of course." Christopher loved this game.

"Christopher," Devoe said with all sincerity in his voice, "I have always believed my introduction to you, when you were an unknown whiz kid in Germany, was predestined. I saw your genius then. And you have never disappointed me."

Christopher rolled his eyes.

Oh brother, predestined. You don't even know the half of it, Devoe.

"Thank you, sir, I really appreciate your faith in me."

"I'm serious. I don't mean to embarrass you son, but I've watched people as you walk into a room. Both men and women stop talking and are drawn by your animal magnetism.

"I'm sure you know what an asset your thick blond hair, blue eyes, and flawless skin are. You would have been a god to Hitler."

The hate swelled up in Christopher.

What a fool!

"You're too kind, Mr. Devoe, thank you. We'll talk soon. I'm sure."

Josh adjusted himself in his broadcaster's chair and adjusted his headset and microphone—liking everything just so before he went on the air.

"Shalom, friends and foe across the fruity plain." Josh's strong voice echoed through the airwaves around the world. "It's a great day, and we've got a great show for you. Here's the phone number if you want to be on the program today, 816510.

"DA-DA-LUP, DA-DA-LUP, DA-DA-LUP....big news today is the scheduled placement of the cornerstone for the new Temple in the Western Wall Plaza. My staff here tells me the faithful of the Temple Mount will be placing the stone on the tenth day of Nisan." Josh rattled his papers.

"Also, let's talk about the unexpected news of the appointment of Christopher Heinman, world president, instead of one of the three other men that many thought would get the post, and we'll have your calls next. Don't go away."

Josh took off his headset, leaned back in his chair, and smiled at Ariel, who recently had become a frequent guest in the studio. "What do you know of Christopher Heinman?" he asked.

"Not a lot, which makes me uneasy." She crossed her arms. "He appeared out of the blue not long ago offering financial support of the new Temple. I understand his parents are deceased, and his grandparents were victims of Dachau. He's not married and seems to have unlimited funds at his disposal."

"Hum." Josh pondered as Thadd motioned him the start of the next segment.

"We're starting the last hour of broadcast excellence. Now who's next on this program? Hello, David from Tel Aviv."

"Shalom, Josh. I've been listening to you for the past weeks, and you appear to be an honest man. I wanted to ask you a question."

"Thank you, David. What's your question?"

"Well, with the rebuilding of the Temple, I was wondering if you see these things pointing to the coming of the Messiah."

Josh expelled a deep breath. "Wow, David, that's a difficult question. I'm not a rabbi, and I haven't done much study of prophecy. However, I do believe in the return of the Messiah. I also believe there will be a false Messiah who will set up a oneworld government." Josh thumbed the desk.

"There are also a lot of things happening in the world today that frighten me such as the major push toward communism in the United States. Anyway, thanks for the call, David...back in a moment."

Josh was visibly shaken as they cut to commercial break. "What's wrong?" Ariel asked.

"I hate those kinds of calls. I used to hate them because I didn't believe that stuff. Now I hate them because I haven't studied it." Josh absentmindedly patted the desk top. "I've always prided myself on being on the cutting edge of information, but prophecy is not that easy to understand. And I don't have a mentor to help me with it."

"I can introduce you to Rabbi Elijah Tzur," Ariel offered.

"Who is he?"

"An old friend of the family. He's published several commentaries on the Messiah." Their conversation was interrupted by the announcer's start of the next segment.

"You're listening to the DIA Network. Next Josh Cohen."

Josh charged into the next segment. "All right, very quickly here, before we go back to phone calls. The European Community has won in its push for a World Trade Agreement, and now the world is changing to a common currency. A common money but different colors. And get this, folks, the United States money is pink. PINK! Can you believe that? Now they've got a bunch of pinko women running the country who have chosen the color pink. Why are you laughing, Eli?" Josh chuckled at the expression on his call screener's face. "At least Israel was smart enough to choose blue.

"Okay, back to the phones. Hello, Dedi in Haifa."

"Hi, Josh. It's nice to finally talk to you."

"I'm glad you called, Dedi."

"I enjoyed your show when I was a student in the United States."

"Oh, really, where did you attend school?" Josh asked.

"Harvard," she said proudly, "and while I was there I had several professors who heaped praises on the work of the Trilateral Commission and the Council on Foreign Relations for bringing about a oneworld system."

She rushed on, "I feel the reason you're seeing this move toward socialism in the United States is due to the influence of these organizations."

"You may be right, Dedi, and of course these groups are funded by large tax-exempt foundations such as the Ford, Carnegie, and Rockefeller Foundations. But let's not forget dear ole Bob Wells, the man who ultimately ushered us into this era of socialism. The man who single-handedly destroyed the Bill of Rights. The man who in the name of national security took away the right to bear arms. The man who in the name of education reforms took away the rights of parents to ensure the education of their children and instead gave us a smart card guaranteed to provide every holder of a "Certificate of Mastery" a job. The man who in the name of justice removed the right to appeal in cases where evidence had been suppressed. And the man who removed the right of Habeas Corpus, trial by jury, if you please. The man who allowed the government to use secret evidence against U.S. citizens. The man who was used as a pawn by the Devil himself. And here I sit. We're out of time, folks. See ya tomorrow."

Josh tossed aside his headset. "I get mad just thinking about that pinko commie."

"So, when do you want to meet Rabbi Tzur?" Ariel searched for a topic to get Josh's mind off his last caller. "Judging the number of calls you got regarding the future of the Holy Land, I'd say your show is taking a turn from the political to the prophetic."

"Oh no," he whined. "I don't know prophecy. How can I possibly tie in the events of the day with what was prophesied thousands of years ago?"

Devoe shrugged off economic doomsday sayers warning of a monetary collapse. He put the morning paper down. He knew what had been planned by the inner circle and was pleased with the progress.

The government no longer offered aid to stricken states ravaged by nature and rioters. Wall Street attempted a tap dance to avoid another Black Monday. One large bank after another closed.

The final blow came when Chase Manhattan, the largest credit card lender, canceled its credit card division and demanded immediate payment on all accounts. The country erupted in panic. Wall Street reeled from the blow. The Dow, trading at 4480, dropped 3700 points to settle at 780. Americans steeled themselves for a disaster, unparalleled in history.

News of the crash spread like a wind-fed wildfire, creating a deep dark hopelessness in the people on Wall Street.

But enough of that. Devoe could hardly wait for this afternoon's emergency meeting of the UN and what was to come.

As New York lay blanketed under the worst snowstorm in history, the U.N. general assembly gathered together, after a 24-hour notice, for the emergency meeting called by new Secretary General, Ford Devoe.

The large hall was packed with a wide variety of peoples—men and women in traditional costume and the latest designer fashion—from white to every color on the flesh chart and sounding something like what ancient Babel sounded after the language barrier appeared.

"Gentleman, it's an honor to be standing before you as your general secretary. I appreciate the trouble each of you took getting here on such short notice and in these severe weather conditions—so much for global warming," he chuckled, then cleared his throat to fill the silence.

"Ah hum... most of you are probably aware of the serious economic crisis facing the United States. To remove any perceived conflict of interest, in my being American, I've asked Christopher Heinman, the new world president to address you."

Christopher relished the standing ovation. "Thank you, thank you." He let the applause die down. "I'm grateful for the opportunity to speak before you, and to address the grave matter that threatens our globe. As most of you are aware, the United States is bankrupt."

A hush descended on the room. He continued, "This is due, in part, to natural disasters that have plagued the world these previous months, and more tragically, the crash of Wall Street. Obviously this throws the whole world into a state of uncertainty.

"In past years, the U.S. has borrowed heavily from the Japanese and the Germans. With the World Trade Agreement now in effect and with a common currency circling the globe, we cannot afford to let this tragedy destroy the dreams of a oneworld system. If we can't come to an agreement today, I would suggest that each of you be prepared to go back to your respective countries and tell your people to prepare themselves for a worldwide depression. Picture in your mind the hysteria that will rage. Picture the deadly runs on your financial institutions, the explosion of crime, mass demonstrations in the streets, and possible execution of your leaders. Basically, it could be the end of life as we know it."

The assembly exploded into an avalanche of confusing sounds and languages. For fifteen minutes, Christopher watched the expressions of anger and fear expose the emotions of the most powerful men representing world governments.

"Gentlemen, I don't present you with this scenario to frighten you. What I see before us is an opportunity to achieve our ultimate dream. In saving the United States from financial ruin, we also save ourselves. The World Trade Agreement has set up a world currency. What I would suggest is utilizing the World Bank in Brussels. This bank is equipped to handle and initiate a cashless method of debits and credits, thus avoiding the inevitable hyper-inflation that would result with the printing of additional currency. Putting more money into circulation would destroy the world's economy as sure as it would destroy the economies of the individual nations if they were to print the money they needed just to pay the interest on their debt. Gentleman," he reminded them, "if one of our member nations defaults, we all go down with him."

The room once again burst into a frenzy of activity. Christopher sat down to ride out the storm, realizing this was what he'd been preparing for all his life.

Being the leader of a world power had its perks.

Emily turned off the private monitor in her office. She let out a sighed of relief. The UN vote to consolidate the world currency into the cashless method of credit and debit had passed.

Hopefully now the news from the World Bank would replace the graphic media stories of race riots, pillage, and long food lines in the major U.S. cities. Hundreds of people had died in the streets from the violence that broke out the day the stock market crashed.

Christopher is certainly a cool operator, she thought. *A fine male specimen, too.*

Her mind wandered as she daydreamed of a future tryst with the world president.

The lines stretching out the doors of every bank in the country were unbelievable. The masses were giddy with the prospects of an instant gift of $1,000.00. Detailed and personal forms were completed without question, and the tiny computer chip that contained everything including each individual's life story, was quickly and easily implanted on hand or forehead.

The masses eagerly opened accounts in the World Bank and embraced the citizenship in the world government. No one seemed to care where that large chunk of money was going to come from?

Josh threw down the *Wall Street Journal* and purposefully stepped on it as he made his way to the kitchen.

Come on, can't even the Wall Street Journal uncover the truth anymore.

He grabbed a bottled tea from the refrigerator.

They've done it. Devoe and his goons have finally suckered the people of America. History books can now record the "Fall of the Great Republic."

News articles varied in detail and length but the information was the same. "Citizenship will be conferred after implantation of a computer chip that will contain the customer's account number. A public 'Pledge of Allegiance' will be performed at The World Church of Peace facilities around the world in approximately six to nine weeks. Pope Simon Peter will lead the pledge, via satellite, from Jerusalem.

Devoe grew giddy over the millions of dollars that piled up in his overseas account. Christopher's suggestion a couple years back to patent the chip was brilliant.

The media made him sound altruistic with their claims that it would be the single most important factor in ridding the earth of crime.

The chip, they praised, would eliminate theft of money, illegal transfer of goods and services, and it would reform all social programs. No longer would welfare recipients be able to double-dip the government. Tax fraud would be a thing of the past, and with these reforms, citizens should look for a reduction in taxes across the board.

The world praised the names of Christopher Heinman and Ford Devoe. Now he was free to work on his deal with Joni Rains.

Harry, anticipating the inevitable economic collapse, had liquidated his portfolio before the rapture and paid off the mortgage on his ranch in Colorado. Living in the corruption of mankind had been a real battle.

Alone and driven by work, he had avoided weekends and vacations. Life had held little meaning for him, and death held little fear. In the darkest of those days, poetry gave him an outlet to vent his frustration and anger at mankind's depravation. Now he thanked God for sparing his soul from an eternity in hell.

He walked out to the carport with another load of supplies. He lowered the tailgate of his brown Blazer and realized how long it had been since he had washed it—once a weekly event now gone by the wayside. He sighed.

He raised a carpeted panel, revealing the hidden cargo bay. He studied the four shovels, three rakes, and five hoes the group had been able to gather. Simple gardening items had become a hot commodity. The typical scene around town had begun resembling shades of the Great Depression with long lines at the welfare agency, employment commission, and grocery stores that were no longer stocked with even the barest of necessities.

The shipping industry had come to a standstill due to the escalating price of gasoline. What food produce was not damaged by violent outbreaks of hail or flooding or not destroyed from pestilence rotted in the fields.

The pressures of staying nameless and faceless in a society suddenly scrutinizing every facet of your life had begun to weigh heavily on Harry's mind. He worried not so much about his own safety, but for the safety of others in the group, especially after the two run-ins with the SSS.

Harry jumped at the sound of his cordless phone. "Hello," he said.

"Harry, it's Marilyn." Her voice cracked with emotion. "I just got a call from Stan... Donna and Kevin have been picked up and are being held downtown."

"What on earth for?" Harry already knew the answer.

"They were witnessing to a friend on campus. Someone overheard and turned them in to campus security." Marilyn began to cry.

"I'll be over in a minute. Call Tommy and the others and tell them to meet at your house." Harry jumped in the car, fumbling with the keys. After unsuccessful tries to start the car with the wrong key, he slammed against the steering wheel. "Get behind me, Satan," he shouted.

When Harry arrived, the others were already there. A somber spirit filled the air. The women were in the living room praying. Stan and Tommy were whispering in the kitchen.

"It doesn't look good," Tommy said as he grabbed Harry on the shoulder with a greeting.

"Has anyone been able to talk to them on the phone?" Harry asked.

"No," Stan replied. "Kevin was able to make that one call, but since then we've been unable to reach them." The men stopped talking as the women walked into the kitchen.

"I'm going downtown to act as council for them," Janet said.

"But you're a political attorney," Harry said, hoping to dissuade her from going downtown. "What do you know about criminal law?"

"Law is law, and as far as I know, the judicial system in this country is still operating even if nothing else is," Janet insisted.

"I'll drive you," Stan volunteered.

"Thanks." Janet grabbed her Gucci bag off the counter.

"Be careful." Sally placed her hands together and up to her lips as she watched Stan and Janet walk to the car.

Janet was shocked to see the deprivation and crime on the streets as they drove downtown. This part of town had always been seedy at night, but now evil boldly displayed itself, no longer hiding from the daylight. Janet locked her door and glanced at Stan, wondering how he had been brave enough to continuing working in law enforcement.

Stan slowly brought his brown Buick to a stop in front of the SSS station. "You try to see Donna and Kevin. I'll go through the back and act as if I'm coming on duty. Maybe I can find out something the department won't tell you." Stan leaned over and squeezed her arm. "Be careful."

She saw the concern in his eyes. "I will."

Smoke and filthy language assaulted Janet as she pushed open the heavy door. She hadn't seen so much activity in one place since before the stock market crash.

Crime must be a booming business, she thought to herself. Janet approached the desk sergeant. "Excuse me, I'm here to see Kevin Mills and Donna Carter, please. I'm their attorney."

"Just a minute, lady. Can't you see I'm busy," he growled.

Janet stepped back from his offensive breath.

"You attorneys think you're so almighty important, too good to wait." He glared at her. "What slimeballs you here to get out?"

"I'm here to see Kevin Mills and Donna Carter. They're not criminals. They've been detained by mistake," she assured him.

"Don't know nothin' 'bout that, lady." He punched their names into his data bank. "We don't get too many in here by mistake. Looks like you're too late. They've been transferred." He sneered in disgust as he continued reading. "Seems to me like they're getting just what they deserve. Says here they're charged with a hate crime, terrorizing some foreign exchange student from Egypt, telling him their God was the only true God. What sadists. They'll burn for that."

"What are you talking about?" Janet shouted. "I'm their attorney. I demand to see them." She leaned toward his desk.

"Get outta my face. They've been charged with violation of the UN Genocide Treaty. Those charges are addressed by the World Court, and there's nothing you or anyone else is going to do about it."

Tears threatened Janet as she pulled the door open to leave, only to be abruptly knocked against the wall. Clearing the cobwebs from her pounding head, she watched a large, dirty man stumble through the door, followed closely by an SSS officer. "Hey, sweet mamma." A horrid smell penetrated Janet's senses as the fat, dirty man drew closer. "How 'bout you'n me getting together a little later." He grabbed for her arm.

"Get away." She recoiled in horror.

The SSS officer burst out laughing. "He'll be out in a couple of hours, princess, if you want to wait around. Come on, 'killer.'" They moved toward the desk sergeant and Janet burst through the door.

"Janet," Stan called out, seeing her rush from the building, "over here."

She searched for his voice, finally seeing his head peeking out around the corner.

"Thank goodness," she said under her breath and hurried over to the car. "It's awful in there. She slammed the car door. "Did you have any better luck finding out where they are than I did?"

Stan didn't answer.

Joni reached over for the phone. Her hand lingered in mid-air, as if creating the courage to call Ford Devoe again. She wondered if their first conversation had made a difference. Emily continued to grow more demanding by the day. A constant threat of expulsion hung over the head of all White House personnel.

She knew Emily and Devoe could barely stand to be in the same building. Two egos their size couldn't fit in the same room.

Joni closed her eyes, picturing herself as Ms. President.

Why not? she thought. *And while I'm at it, Devoe could probably do something about Josh Cohen, too. Maybe he could do them at the same place.*

Joni pictured in her mind Emily and Josh Cohen dying together.

The world would be a better place, I'm sure.

She laughed.

10

"Then shall they deliver you up to be afflicted,
and shall kill you;
and ye shall be hated of all nations
for my name's sake."
(Matthew 24:9)

The occupants of the prison bus sat huddled together. Day turned into night and night into day as they traveled across the Texas plains toward Arizona. The drive through New Mexico brought the cold mountain air creeping in through broken windows. The old bus heater did little more than warm the driver's knees.

As the numbing effect of the situation wore off, a comforting spirit descended on the prisoners. A soft soulful melody floated up from the back as two black women harmonized. Little by little people joined in, until the bus was bursting with praise. Even Ed, the bus driver, couldn't stop his foot from keeping time with the music.

"This is certainly the strangest bus load of prisoners I've ever transported," Ed said to his assistant officer. It was hard trying to visualize these people committing hate crimes against anyone. Ed had been offered this new post because of the reputation he'd built up of being the biggest, meanest, and ugliest cop on the force. He had appeared before the review board several times. Being charged with brutality had become common for him. He had always been cleared of the charges, usually because the defendants had changed their stories after being visited by one of Ed's friends. Ed's supervisor had warned him of the severity of the crimes committed by the people he would be transporting. They were to be treated like and considered to be the most dangerous criminals he had ever been in contact with.

He had arrived at the station, in baited anticipation, of this first prison run to the new Regional Detention Center in Arizona. He'd started the morning off right, fighting with his girlfriend.

Ed's supervisor recognized the expression on Ed's face when he arrived. "Ed, are you ready to get these dredges of human existence to Arizona?"

"Yeah." Ed cracked his knuckles. "What are most of them in for? Murder?"

"Worse than murder, man. These people broke international law. They'll be tried by the World Judge and, from what I understand, it'll be some time before the judge can get to the States due to the number of cases she's having to hear in Europe. No need to worry about these jokers getting out early due to overcrowding," the supervisor chuckled. "They'll be lucky if they're still alive and kicking by the time she gets around to the good ole U.S.-of-A."

Ed drifted back to the joyful sound emanating from his prisoners—criminals he'd been told who were the worst of the worst. He looked in his rearview mirror at their faces and decided someone had made a bad mistake.

It was the "big game" A&M vs. UT weekend in Austin, Texas. College football at its finest. Harry looked down from his fourth-story office window at the parade below. Even with the current economic situation, diehard UT fans continued the parade's tradition. As the University of Texas 'Gay Club' danced past, Harry's attention was captured by a group of black boys dressed in orange. He studied them as they strolled around from the alley, noticing the bats they carelessly swung. As he continued to watch, his skin became clammy and flushed. His muscles tightened. His anger burst forth as he watched the gang begin to swing the bats indiscriminately. An elderly white man was knocked to the ground. The crowd scattered, startling the parade participants as people ran into the street. Women rushed their children to safety in the nearest building.

The smell of fear energized the gang members and they continued their attack. The sidewalk became stained with the blood of their victims.

Harry's fists clenched as he watched a young Hispanic girl with a baby stroller being chased through the crowd. She reached the entrance of the office building across the street. She grabbed for the door as the building security officer turned the lock. Harry watched her frantic attempts to get in. He froze in horror as the security man backed up, refusing to help as the glass shattered and the young mother's blood oozed down the door.

"You are now listening to the DIA Network. Stay tuned for Josh Cohen, next." Thadd, rushing to prepare for the program was distracted by a loud ruckus in the outer hall.

"Go find out what's going on out there," he instructed Joey, his young Palestinian assistant.

Thadd clued Josh in.

"Shalom, Shalom aleichem, peace be unto you, my friends. This is Josh Cohen coming to you live from Jerusalem, the holy international city. We've got lots to talk about today. The upcoming World Citizen Day celebration, the signing of the World Constitution at UN headquarters, soon to be called World Headquarters, in New York, and your calls next." Josh reached for his cigar. "What's going on in there?" Josh hollered at the break, seeing the staff gathered around Joey, whose skinny arms whipped through the air.

"The whole building's in an uproar, Josh," Thadd exclaimed. "The Vatican and Palestinian embassies are causing a commotion over two old men who just appeared at the Wailing Wall."

"So what's the big deal?" Josh questioned.

"These old codgers are shouting, 'Repent Israel, the Kingdom of the Lord is at hand.'" Thadd laughed nervously.

Chills ran up Josh's back as he recalled the scripture in Revelation regarding the two witnesses.

The three-hour show seemed to drag on endlessly for Josh. He could hardly wait to get down to the Wailing Wall and check out the two prophets for himself.

The recent world events spurred Tommy's small Bible study group on. Their mood had been bleak after the arrests of Donna and Kevin. Janet and Stan had followed up on every lead but to no avail. They all struggled with the thought of leaving their two friends behind, but the Lord moved forward their plans to move to Harry's ranch in Colorado.

Tears escaped as Sally gingerly ran her hands over the elegant evening dresses that lined her deep, spacious closet. Three pairs of jeans, three T-shirts, two sweatshirts, underclothes, a wind breaker, and one pair of tennis shoes stuffed the canvas duffel bag, hanging at her side.

She walked to the front door, then turned and looked once more around the room. Her eyes stopped on the faces of her husband and small daughter, framed lovingly in a crème-colored porcelain heart.

"It won't be long, my darlings," she whispered and shut the door.

The sun slowly made its way up as Sally backed her beige suburban out of the driveway for the last time. Tears streamed down her face, her heart breaking as she questioned her resolve to leave everything behind.

This is almost as bad as facing the reality of the accident, she thought to herself.

She drove down the street with her window down and breathed in the crisp morning air. Her mind drifted back over the first few years after her loss—years she'd spent living in despair, cursing God every waking moment, her mind unable to comprehend why He would take her precious Paul and Amy at the hands of a drunk.

Sally had cursed Him for leaving her alive, yet at the same time, ripping her heart out. After cursing God, she'd cursed the little Bible Church that drew Paul every Sunday morning to its doors. She blamed herself for allowing Paul to take her beautiful Amy to church with him. Every night, after the curses were spent, she'd cry herself to sleep.

The pastor of Paul's church tried for months after the accident to comfort Sally, but the pain and bitterness burned too deeply. It took the rapture to finally break Satan's grip on her heart.

After the funeral, months went by without her giving much thought to Paul's pastor, or that small church, until the Sunday following the rapture.

About 9:30 that morning she drove down the tree-lined street on her way to the donut shop. As she passed, it struck her odd that no cars were faithfully parked in the church's small parking lot. She swerved into the lot and parked her car. She walked up to the large, walnut-stained double doors and placed her slender hand on the large handle.

"It's locked," came a slurred voice behind her. Startled, she whirled around. Immediately horrified, she realized she was face-to-face with the monster who killed her precious family. "Oh, God," she cried in anguish, falling to the ground unconscious. A strong odor of bourbon jolted her awake.

"Wake up, ma'am. I didn't mean to scare you. I'm so sorry." The man sobbed. He stood up to leave, and Sally grabbed his arm, her curiosity overcoming her hatred.

"Where are they?" she whispered.

"Gone," he whimpered. "To heaven. All of them, my family, wife, kids, and the people who used to come here."

"How do you know?" She didn't believe this drunken murderer.

"Reverend Davis use to talk a lot 'bout the rapture. Jesus was coming to take all the Christians to heaven with Him."

"You were a member of this church?" she asked surprised.

"No." He sadly shook his head. "I used to hang around the doors and listen, waitin' on Charlotte and the kids. Reverend Davis was nice to me. He urged me to come in, but I was too ashamed at what I done, who I was. Didn't think God could forgive someone like me." He hung his head and started to leave again.

"Wait," Sally cried, strangely drawn to this man. "If they've all been taken to heaven, why are you still hanging around here?"

"I don't really know," he shrugged.

Sally slowed her white suburban, reliving the past as she drove by that small, now deserted church building. She looked at the very spot where the Lord had brought her to confront the past. Where she'd faced the focus of her hatred—a middle-aged man named Randy, marriage on the rocks, a slave to the bottle, left behind and haunting a church building, searching for a purpose. That Sunday morning, two years ago, the Lord had cleansed the bitterness and hate and washed away the guilt that followed. Sally stared at the broken remnants of stained-glass windows and tall weeds, and then faced forward and drove on by. "Thank you, Lord," she whispered, knowing He knew the heart-felt words she couldn't voice.

She wiped her tears and pulled up to the automatic teller machine. Running low on cash, she decided to withdraw the last $200 in her checking account.

She walked into the small glass booth and placed her ATM card in the machine. The ominous sound of the door swing open behind her forced her to swing around as she finished her transaction. Her heart leaped, staring into the face of evil.

"Looky, what we've got here, Spike. A pretty filly with long brown legs and a mane of thick red hair." A skinny hand with unkempt finger nails reached out to caress her cheek.

She backed up. The cold of the brick wall penetrated her silk blouse.

"Come on, honey, don't be shy. Me and Spike won't hurt ya."

"She'd make a nice addition to your herd, Spike. You could use some new blood in that bunch of old nags you've got now."

He turned to look at his companion. She seized her only opportunity for escape and bolted for the door. Caught off guard, the two men stumbled and fell to the ground. Sally desperately rushed to her Suburban. In her terror, she failed to notice the curb guard and tripped, sailing into the flowerbed. Excruciating pain shot through her leg. She dug her manicured nails into the damp earth, crushing the tiny white flowers planted there. Dirty tennis shoes stopped beside her. She looked up into the cold, steel black eyes of her assailant.

"Looks like she's down, Spike." He squatted to Sally's level. "What do you think?" he asked, as if she was going to answer him. "You know what happens to injured horses at the track."

He stood up and tossed the butt of his cigarette at her. "This filly's no good to us with a broken leg, Spike. Guess we better take her money. She won't be needing it anymore."

The large branches of the oak tree shaded the area from the bright morning sun. Singing birds played among the leaves. The traffic of I-35 rushed by, and a gentle breeze stroked Sally's brow. Time stood still as Sally closed her eyes.

"I'm coming, baby," she whispered as the roar of gunshot shattered the air.

The world seemed to fall into step with Christopher and his new policies. The masses were the first to register for world citizenship and the $1,000.00 immediate World Bank credit. With the reduction of taxes and the open access to all markets, the earth appeared to rotate with a flurry of economic activity.

The stabilization of world markets ended riots and civil unrest. Without the "underprivileged and disadvantaged" to rally behind, radical warlords and dictators lost any hold they otherwise had over their countrymen. The world began to proclaim Christopher a savior.

Devoe leaned back in his chair and propped his polished alligator boots up on his desk. He relished the thought of the millions of dollars that his new world government account would generate. Money just poured into his pocket all because of that tiny computer chip. He envisioned the hordes of people lining up at clinics around the world and having it implanted in their hand or forehead. The strange sequence of numbers Christopher wanted each chip to contain still puzzled him. *But what the heck! Money talks and Christopher has access to plenty of it.*

Having access to the world government through Christopher made all the difference in DCI securing the contract for the small chip. Next would come the order for additional computer scanners to read the chip and then the data processing ability to track and locate every individual on the planet through the new satellite soon to be launched. Devoe rubbed his hands together.

Of course there's the critic of the chip. The mouth himself, Josh Cohen, voicing his concerns of the new world citizenship and my part in the implementation of the world computer system. Devoe swore.

Josh had been a thorn in his side since the '92 election campaign.

It's time to do away with that mouthpiece.

Devoe schemed. *I'll make him sorry he ever tried to play ball with the big boys. Israel can't protect him any better than his millions of mind-numb robot listeners in the U.S. could protect him.* Devoe gazed out his office window, overlooking the activity of the tiny impotent beings below him.

I'm in the driver's chair now, he pondered. *No one can keep me from going all the way to the top.*

Next stop, the world presidency.

"Greetings fellow chit-chatters across the global boardwalk of life. The word for today is 'Repent, for the Kingdom of the Lord is at hand.' That's right, folks. Front page of the "Jerusalem Post." Pictured underneath are the two unique characters in black, bringing that message and causing quite a stir at the Wailing Wall. Such a stir, in fact, that Pope Simon Peter and the World Church have issued a statement calling these two old men heretics and hatemongers who deserve to be punished for their crimes." Josh drummed his table for emphasis.

"Their message is drawing a scathing review, not to mention their dress." Josh drummed his table again. "I saw them for myself last evening. These two, whom some are proclaiming prophets, are dressed in sackcloth. Which by the way, I'm told, is the dress of one in mourning. Is there a symbolic message in their dress?

"And we've gotten word of a strange new plague—people breaking out in boils. Could it be a result of a foreign object being placed under the skin, compliments of Ford Devoe. And," he continued, "news of recent struggles in South Africa and bizarre rat attacks in India. Also, mounting nuclear tension between North and South Korea. Could it be that our knight in shining armor, Mr. World President himself is not the peacemaker many have idolized him to be? We'll be right back, folks. Lots to talk about. Don't go away." Josh lit his cigar.

"You know who the orthodox Jews are saying those two men are, don't you?" Thadd raised his eyebrows and smiled mischievously.

"You bet," Josh assured him. "They're the two guys God sent to foretell the second coming of the Messiah.

"I believe," Josh retorted, "the Bible hints that they're Elijah and Moses."

"Moses! You're kidding. No way. The other guy is Enoch. And, it's the first coming of the Messiah.

Who do you think the Messiah is?" Thadd asked. Excitement escaping from his every pore.

Josh studied his young producer, who he'd recently discovered was a member of the Temple Faithful Group, the group known for trying, at least once a year, to place the corner stone on the Temple Mount.

"I'll have to think on it. I'm not a prophecy expert." Josh wasn't about to get into a discussion with Thadd regarding the Antichrist.

Josh put his cigar down as the 'On the Air' green light flashed on. "DA-DA-LUP, DA-DA-LUP, DA-DA-LUP, and now, folks, a stupidity update. As we all know, India has been troubled with famine and a caste war in recent months. These combined with bubonic plague have ravaged the country claiming close to twelve million lives. And yet, you're not going to believe this, folks. The government of India has succumbed to pressure from the UN's animal rights activists, protesting the country's efforts to rid Calcutta and Bombay of the estimated combined rat population of four billion." Josh pounded his table. "Do these idiots not realize it's the rat fleas that are causing these people to suffer horrible deaths." Josh shuffled his papers.

"Now get this, today Reuters International News Service is running a story of bizarre, unexplained attacks on pedestrians by large rats. India has always had four and five pound rats, but they stayed hidden. They're night creatures. Folks, think about it." Josh drummed his thumb on the table. "What has brought these large monsters out into the daylight?"

An uncontrolled shiver ran up Josh's back talking about it. "The report goes on to tell the story of one lady who was rushed to the hospital, legs mutilated, from being attacked on her way home from the market. Fortunately for her, hunters a block down heard the screams and rushed to her aid, probably saving her life."

Josh paused to emphasize his point. "And now, folks, the UN has outlawed the slingshot-type weapon and put in jail the men who killed the three six-pound rats as they viciously attacked this innocent woman. I've gotta take a break, folks. Stay tuned for the last hour. Don't go away."

11

"Blessed are ye when men shall hate you,
and when they shall separate you
from their company,
and shall reproach you,
and cast out your name as evil,
for the Son of Man's sake.
Rejoice in that day, and leap for joy;
for behold your reward is great in heaven;
for in like manner did their fathers
unto the prophets."
(Luke 6:22, 23).

The grueling journey began taking its toll on the fifteen prisoners. Even the prison transporter, Ed, tough as he was, suffered the effects of the three-day, mandatory non-stop drive to the Arizona Detention Center.

"Kevin, I'm so frightened." Donna reached over and wrapped her arm around Kevin's as tight as her chains would allow. "What do you think's going to happen to us?" Her voice quivered.

"I don't know, Babe. But I do know God is in control." He squeezed her hand.

Suddenly, a loud explosion ripped through the air and the bus pitched to the left side. Everyone screamed as shards of broken glass slammed through the air.

The stillness of the desert was shattered by the ton of yellow metal hurdling down the embankment.

Just as suddenly, the noise stopped and the dust settled. The large tires on the bus spun to a halt.

Donna's eyes fluttered. Sounds of loud moaning woke her up. She raised her hand to still the pounding of her head. Blood trickled out from her thick brown hair, staining her fingertips dark red. She slowly moved her legs, freeing them from an unknown burden.

"Kevin," she whispered. Her mind flashed back to the sound of the blowout. She forced herself awake, realizing the bus had somersaulted off the treacherous winding road.

"Kevin," she said louder.

Donna struggled to her knees, bracing herself with the seat, her mind unprepared for the scene that confronted her. Broken bodies were tossed across seats or propelled through windows, landing among the rocks. The bus driver's short legs stuck out under the side window, his upper body crushed and hidden beneath the bus.

The other prison guard's bloodied face pressed against the wire cage that separated the prisoners from the front cab.

A sob caught in Donna's throat. "Kevin?" she said again, trying to wipe the blood from her eyes as she searched the bus. A voice from the back seized Donna's attention.

"Help." A thin black hand reached around and gripped the side of the backseat.

Donna stumbled over bodies, making her way to the back, checking each barrier as she went, looking for Kevin.

"Oh, God!" Donna gasped, peering behind the seat and seeing a stark, white leg bone protruding grotesquely through the dark, bloodied skin.

"It's okay, sweetie... I'm a nurse," the woman said, taking a deep breath. "Just help me out of the bus and everything will be all right."

Donna flinched, seeing the pain on the woman's face, as she helped her up. They slowly made their way over seats and bodies to the middle of the bus as it teetered against a boulder.

Donna steadied the injured woman by a broken window, and, placing her hands to avoid broken glass, crawled out. She reached back in to pull the woman out. The bus began to rock from the motion of the two women. A burst of adrenaline gave Donna the strength she needed to pull the woman free.

Donna collapsed in the brush, her energy spent. She glanced down and discovered the woman unconscious. *She's better off*, she thought.

Blood, pulsating from the woman's broken leg, stained the dirt around her. Donna ripped off her slip and quickly tightened a tourniquet above the woman's knee.

Cries for help from other wounded drew Donna's attention. She wiped the sweat out of her eyes and stumbled back to the bus. A strong odor of gas gave her a fright. *Dear God,* she prayed, *please don't let this bus catch fire.*

Donna helped those still alive out of the bus and then scrambled up the side of the embankment. *I've got to get help,* she thought as panic rose to her chest. She searched up and down the long stretch of desolate road. Tears formed in her tired, red eyes.

God," she cried, "please help me." Suddenly in the distance she saw the dust of an approaching vehicle. Donna began to wave frantically as it approached.

An old white Ford Pickup pulled up beside her. "What's wrong, child?" asked the elderly man.

Relief flooded through Donna as she gazed into the bright eyes of the kindly old man. As tension rushed out of her muscles, her knees buckled.

The old man jumped out of his truck and picked her up out of the dirt. Stronger than his appearance indicated, he carried Donna around to the passenger side of the truck and gently sat her on the cracked, brown vinyl bench seat. Gently he shut the door. As the engine purred into action, Donna came too.

"Wait," she shouted, placing her hand on his arm as he shifted into drive. "We've got to help those people." Her green eyes filled with tears.

"Don't worry, dear, help is on the way." He studied her eyes for signs of a concussion. "Right now we've got to get you taken care of. That's a nasty cut you've got there." His wrinkled hand lightly touched her forehead. His compassion soothed Donna's fears and squelched the anxiety of the previous two days. A peace descended over her. The hot afternoon sun and rhythm of the truck lulled her into a deep peaceful sleep as it bounced along the back roads of the New Mexico mountains.

Josh moved toward the front of the crowd, trying to get a better look at the two prophets who stood in stark contrast to the stone wall behind them. Long white hair framed their age-old faces. Their voices, deep and strong, carried above the crowd. Their message was the same, "Repent, the Kingdom of God is at hand." Josh noticed the angry group that gathered, high atop the Wailing Wall. He recalled the 1989 riot when rocks, hurled down by angry Palestinians on to the crowd of worshipers below, killed several people.

A soldier of the World Government pushed Josh aside as several officers made their way to the old men. Two blond-headed, high-ranking officers approached the prophets. "Move along, fellows, we can't have you causing a disturbance."

"We are not under your authority, sir."

"Excuse me?" the officer said, incredulous that anyone would dare question the authority of the newly formed World Government. "The Lord our God has given us authority for 1,260 days to proclaim His message to Israel."

"I'm sorry, sir, but you have no authority here, and if you refuse to leave these premises immediately, we'll have to take you in."

One of the officers reached over to nudge the old man along, only to recoil from a burning pain that shot up his arm. "Hey, old man," he yelled, searching his hand for evidence of injury.

The other officer, anticipating a problem reached over to grab the old man's arm and experienced the same burning pain. The crowd became uneasy as red blisters formed on the two officers' hands.

Angered, one of the officers pulled his gun and thrust it into the prophet's stomach. "You will come with us or be shot." As his figure tightened on the trigger, fire ripped out of the heavens and consumed the body of the UN police officer. A hush descended on the crowd. The officers backed off. Palestinians watching from above quickly disbursed.

Josh couldn't believe his eyes.

Two rabbis behind him whispered. "Who do you think they are?" the one asked his companion.

"Elijah, of course. Like the good Book says. And Moses."

"Moses? What good book have you been reading? He's not Moses. There is only one other man who didn't taste the hand of death, and that was Enoch."

"Well, this is the rainy season. Elijah has the power to seal up the heavens and stop the rain. It'll will be interesting to see whether he does or not."

Josh was stunned to hear the two rabbis discussing the prophets.

I've got to ask Ariel the name of that rabbi she wants me to meet.

"Josh." Thadd pushed his way through the uneasy crowd to catch up to his boss. "Enoch and Elijah are acquiring a large following, but I didn't know you were one of them."

"I could say the same for you, Thadd." Josh joked with his young producer, trying to shake off the shock of watching that soldier burn to death.

"I'm here to check out the progress on the Temple. I noticed your car several blocks back and thought you might be here." Thadd shuffled his feet.

"Speaking of the Temple, it is sure going up in a hurry. How are they building it so fast?" Josh looked into Thadd's dark brown eyes and noticed the passion that sprang forth at the mention of the Temple.

"That's a secret," he whispered, "but if you'll keep it between you and me..."

"I can keep a secret. You think just because I'm the godzilla of talk radio that I can't keep a secret?"

"I'm not saying you can't keep a secret, boss. It's just that you're American." Thadd never passed up a chance to chide Josh about his American heritage.

"Okay, Thadd, spill the beans." He enjoyed sparring with his new friend.

"Well..." Thadd pressed his palms to the sides of his jeans. "Since 1986, some friends and I have been quarrying stone with even tzor, or a special stone called Shamir."

"What is tzor?"

"It's flint. We're not allowed to use iron tools to quarry this stone because it would be disrespectful to beat the holy stones used for God's house."

"Are you saying that you and some friends have been shaping stones for the Temple since 1986?" Josh couldn't believe this kid's dedication.

"That's right. In the south of Israel, there's a beautiful place in the desert, called Mitzpe Ramon. The character and color of the stone there is very similar to that of the first and second temples."

"So you're telling me that this Temple was prefabricated, just waiting for the time it could be put in place on the Temple Mount. You surprise me, Thadd. I didn't think there were any dedicated young people left in the world."

Thadd's heart swelled from the praises of this man he had come to admire and respect. "You planning to stay around here much longer?" Thadd asked, noticing a change in the atmosphere of the crowd.

"No, I wouldn't be surprised to see a fight break out in the next few minutes. These prophets aren't mincing words. I doubt they'll be overly popular with the typical bar crowd. We better get out of here before the rocks start flying."

Christopher kept to himself in his free time. He had no desire to share his life's story or to hear someone else's. He had one purpose on this earth and his goal was to focus all his energy toward his success.

He watched the two prophets on the evening news. A burning hatred filled his chest. *How dare they refuse to obey my orders. I have brought peace to this wartorn region. I have eased the burdens of the poor. I have allowed the rebuilding of the Temple. I've ensured a stable economy for peoples around the world. I'll not have them spreading their hatred and lies among my people.* Christopher turned off the TV and picked up the phone. He dialed the pope's private number.

"Hello." Simon Peter stretched his long thin legs in anticipation of the daily call from one of the few who had his direct number.

"Pope Simon Peter, this is Christopher Heinman. I hope I haven't interrupted anything?" Christopher smirked, knowing all about Simon Peter's private life.

"Of course not." Simon Peter slid off the leather couch, cursing the person who had given out his personal phone number to the world president.

"What can I do for you?"

"I want your opinion of the two old men ranting and raving at the Wailing Wall."

Simon Peter spat. "They're heretics—demon-possessed."

Christopher smiled. "So you think their miracles are satanic?"

"Absolutely. A loving God wouldn't inflict His children with the horrible plagues these two have called up from hell." Simon Peter rubbed his hand across the soft fur of his black Persian cat.

"What about all these converts accepting tribal markings?" Christopher had been surprised that these prophets claimed to know the tribes their Jewish followers descended from.

"Black magic," Simon insisted, thinking of his own involvement with it several years ago. "All genealogical records were burned when the Temple was destroyed in AD 70, and..." Simon Peter paused. "Why are you asking me all this? You're Jewish."

"As are you, Joseph Steinem." Silent incrimination saturated the air waves between them.

"But back to our mutual problem. How would you suggest we silence those two mad men?"

"Kill 'em." Simon was through playing games.

"That's a little harsh, don't you think? After all, we are living in a time of peace and brotherly love." Christopher's attempt to mock Simon Peter didn't go unnoticed.

Simon Peter bristled, "What would you suggest?"

"This is your area of expertise, Your... Holiness." Christopher was angry and refused to restrain the sarcasm in his voice.

"I'll see what I can do. Is there anything else we need to discuss?" Simon Peter paced the room.

"Not at this time. I'll be in touch, Your Eminence. Have a pleasant evening." Christopher hung up and stretched back in his plush gray recliner. *I can't trust that fool to get the job done right,* he thought to himself. *I've got to get the crowds away from that wall. Those old men are accumulating too many converts.*

Christopher closed his eyes. A bright light illuminated his mind as he reached deep into his soul. The years of meditation and yoga enabled him go right to the center of his focus.

"Master." He kneeled and bowed before his god.

12

"I saw one of his heads
as if it were wounded to death,
and his deadly wound was healed;
and all the world wondered after the beast.
And they worshiped the dragon
which gave power unto the beast;
and they worshiped the beast, saying,
Who is like the beast?
Who is able to make war with him?"
(Revelation 13:3, 4)

Harry slowly put his car in reverse. The large, white parking space number 33 painted on the wall before him burned itself into his brain.

How strange, he mused, *that everything about this parking space would become so vividly imprinted on my mind as I see it for the last time.*

He pulled out of the complex.

No regrets.

He approached the intersection and began to brake for the traffic signal ahead. He leaned over and pushed in his favorite CD. The voice of Cynthia Clawson filled the car, and he drank in the richness of the melody.

As the brake pedal brought the car to a gentle stop, Harry's foot suddenly slammed to the floor and his body lurched into the steering wheel.

It took him a couple of minutes for his brain to come out of the fog and realize he had been hit from behind. A small trickle of blood ran into his left eye.

Blaring sirens and shouting voices penetrated Harry's dazed senses.

A young man jerked the blazer door open. "Come on, you've got to get out of here."

"What?" Harry stared at him through squinted eyes. "This wasn't my fault. I was hit from behind." Harry stumbled from the car.

"You've been set up." The stranger urged Harry to an old white pickup, idling on the other side of the intersection.

"But..." Harry looked back at his Blazer. "I've got stuff in the back. I can't leave it."

"God will provide. Come on."

The startling words silenced Harry's argument. He turned and followed the young man who was already running across the street.

The two men jumped in the truck and drove through the intersection as a swarm of SSS patrolmen converged on the accident scene.

Harry studied the profile of his rescuer. "Who are you?"

The man looked over and smiled. Harry was taken aback by the brilliance of his blue eyes. For some unknown reason, Harry felt compelled to tell his companion of the small Bible study group's plans to move to Colorado. His words flowed in a steady stream. As his story came to a conclusion, Harry realized the truck had stopped.

He looked up and recognized Stan's house and realized he was standing on the sidewalk. He whirled around to look at the truck and there wasn't a truck. His heart skipped a beat.

Is this all really happening to me? He rubbed his eyes. *Ouch, that hurts.*

Dawn pushed the darkness aside as the sun rose over Jerusalem. Christopher finished his morning meditation, feeling the familiar seeds of boredom begin to take root.

It's time to move on to bigger and better things, he reflected. *My talents are being wasted. I think the masses have been happy with my handouts. It's time they bestowed on me my rightful title.*

He turned on the radio. He'd gotten into the habit of listening to Josh Cohen, although he didn't know why.

"This is a special edition of the Josh Cohen Show, and now from our studio in Jerusalem..."

"Hey, hey, hey, greetings to you chatters across the global boardwalk. Welcome to the DIA World Service coming to you at 29.842 megahertz on the shortwave. It's day 1,220 of the Jerusalem Covenant. Here's the phone number if you want to be on the program today, 816510. We've got lots to talk about. Don't go away." Josh organized the newspaper headlines and the topics he planned to discuss.

"Okay, folks." He crinkled his papers. "This is the day we've been waiting for. The Temple is completed. Rabbi Elijah Tzur has asked Pope Simon Peter to be the guest speaker at the dedication ceremony. World President Christopher Heinman will be the speaker at the banquet, and a host of world dignitaries are honoring us with their presence here this week. And... in the midst of this happy occasion, the three words that put a damper on the scheduled festivities are 'Death, War and Plague.'

"What, Eli, you don't think things are really that bad?" Josh interrupted his monologue to converse with his call screener. "You may be right, Eli. Mr. World President himself says there's too much negative preachin' goin' on, but let me give you a few examples of all that's wrong with this world. The pres has been busy these past months, negotiating one treaty after another. Freedom-loving people around the globe are embroiled in civil war and, as is the case in war, food is in short supply.

To avoid future world-wide panic, the UN will be discussing possible food rationing at the meeting next month. And," Josh paused, "if all this doesn't concern you, today Reuters reports of the alarming outbreak of a mutant strain of the AIDS virus that has virtually wiped out Africa. Gotta break. Back in just a minute." Josh loosened his tie and lit one of his treasured Cuban cigars. Legally buying and smoking Cuban cigars had been one of the perks of living in Israel these last three years.

Thadd signaled the start of the next segment.

"You're tuned to the Josh Cohen program, which is a daily and relentless pursuit of the truth. Now, I realize, friends, I've occupied much of our time with monologue, and so I want to go to the phones. Hello, Derrick in Sidney, Australia."

"Thanks for taking my call. You're the highlight of our day."

"My pleasure, Derrick. What's on your mind."

"Plague and rats. I want to tell you what is happening in Australia with the rats."

"What's that, Derrick?" Josh blew cigar smoke at the ceiling. "Josh, I own a one hundred-acre farm and I grow wheat." The sounds of children playing in the background came through the phone. "Rats are destroying my farm. They've taken over my barn. They've eaten my crop, and they've moved into my house."

"Derrick, we all hear mice in our walls on occasion," Josh assured him.

"You don't understand, Josh. We wake up in the morning with rats in the sheets and droppings on the pillows."

"Derrick, I thought the government had a rat extermination program to help farmers."

"They used to, but UN animal rights activists pushed through a measure to outlaw the program."

"You've got to be kidding." Josh pounded his palm on the table.

"No, Josh, I'm not. We've begged and begged. We've camped on the steps of the farm administration building. We've done everything we could think of. Nothing has helped."

"So what are you going to do, Derrick?"

"We're leaving the farm. We can't pay the mortgage without a crop, and we can't take the emotional stress any longer. Yesterday morning, my wife walked into the kitchen and found our two-year-old daughter munching on a rat's head. That was it. My wife's packing and we're moving to town."

"Wow. Take care of yourself and your family, Derrick." Josh said a silent prayer as Derrick hung up.

"Folks, if there's any animal lovers out there listening to this, I urge you to consider the fact that India has lost two-thirds of its population to bubonic plague, which is carried by rat fleas, and that typhus, also carried by rat fleas, is killing hundreds of millions of people around the world. Don't go away." Josh leaned back, stretching his arms over his head.

Ariel strolled into the studio, her perfume filling the room with spring flowers. Josh looked up from his stack of papers and admired her smart suit and shapely legs. She leaned up against Josh's table and crossed her legs.

"I'll pick you up tonight. The banquet starts at 7:30." She ruffled through his papers.

"Come on, Ariel," Josh pleaded, straightening his paper piles. "You know I don't like these state banquets."

"Lighten up, Josh. We're going to be sitting with Rabbi Tzur. I thought you wanted to meet him." Her full lips teased him with a smile. "Besides, dad wants you there."

"Okay, okay." Josh felt a stirring at her nearness. Thadd's cue of the last hour prevented him from dwelling on it.

The large banquet hall shimmered in the sparkle of magnificent jewels displayed proudly by the elite of society. Waiters in black pants and crisp white shirts hustled around the room refilling wine glasses.

Ariel led Josh through the throngs of dignitaries to their front-row table. Its occupants stood as Ariel approached.

"Gentlemen, I'd like you to meet my guest, Josh Cohen, I'm sure you've all heard his show." The men nodded in affirmation.

"Josh, this is Rabbi Elijah Tzur."

"My pleasure, sir. Ariel speaks often of you." Josh shook his hand.

"And this is Rabbi Meir Deri, previously of New York."

"Nice to meet you, Rabbi. How long have you been in Jerusalem?" Josh asked.

"Long enough to know we're headed for trouble."

Ariel quickly introduced others at the table as the lights dimmed and Ben walked to the podium.

"Shalom, my friends. Tonight, as of old, we hold fast to the truth of the words of the prophets of Israel that all the inhabitants of the world shall enter within the gates of Jerusalem. Each and every nation shall live in it by its own faith. In this spirit, the Knesset of the State of Israel has enacted a law: The places holy to the peoples of all religions shall be protected from any desecration and from any restriction of free access to them. And in this vein, we gather to celebrate the Holy Temple, the Throne of the House of David.

"Tonight we are honored with the presence of our own 'Peacemaker,' Christopher Heinman, world president."

The hall erupted in thunderous applause as Christopher approached the podium.

"Honored guests and friends, thank you for your devotion to this holy city. We all have a responsibility for a better global order. Guarantees of freedom of conscience and religion are necessary, but they cannot stand in the way of values, convictions and norms that are valid for all humans. Therefore, I call on each and everyone tonight to pledge your allegiance not only to unity but to the elimination of aggression and hatred in the name of religion."

The audience, vividly reminded of the despised two prophets, exploded in applause. Josh gawked in dismay at Christopher's blatant attack on freedom. Adoring eyes around the room focused on the exquisite picture Christopher made. The light bounced off his hair, creating a halo-like glow. Behind him, the mural of the new Temple radiated at Christopher's presence.

This is it, Josh thought. *I fled from growing tyranny in the United States. Where will I go now? I've become the epitome of a man without a country. What team will I root for? Lord, it looks like it's come down to just you and that adversary of old, the Devil.* Josh whirled around at the loud explosion of gunfire. He backed up, horrified at the sight of Rabbi Deri, standing next to him, holding the discharged .38 special.

A throng of soldiers invaded their table. Rabbi Deri was grabbed from all sides and the gun yanked from his hand. Josh and Ariel were separated by the onslaught of military and medical personnel rushing to the podium. A path cleared as Christopher was carried out on a stretcher. Josh headed for the exit as women and men all around him openly sobbed.

Dignitaries whispered among themselves. Josh caught a glimpse of Emily Wells, Joni Rains, and Ford Devoe talking at his left. He turned, too late to avoid being seen.

"You!" Emily screeched, clawing through the crowd.

Devoe stepped back so he would not get caught on film by the media that quickly gathered.

"This is all your fault. You hatemonger. You were at that murderer's table."

"Come on, Josh." Ariel appeared beside him, tugging on his large frame as people began to congregate around them.

"Don't try and run away this time, Josh Cohen. I'm going to make sure people know what kind of a bigot and racist you really are." Emily's face distorted with rage as she shouted obscenities.

Christopher was rushed to Hadassah Hospital, where he was pronounced dead on arrival. The *Jerusalem Post* bantered the morning paper with "Rabbi Kills 'PeaceMaker'!"

The global media echoed the sentiment, "Christopher Heinman, heralded by leaders of every country as the greatest peacemaker in history, was assassinated yesterday. He was widely acclaimed as the most brilliant mind of the millennium. The loss in world leadership cannot be measured. No other man has done more to solve the problems of the world and to unify nations." The world shifted into mourning. Stock markets reeled from the blow and threatened worldwide economic collapse.

Josh fought a raging battle brewing in his mind as his staff prepared for the day's program.

Thadd and Eli had heard on the radio early that morning of the scene President Wells created the previous evening. Calls had started pouring in two hours before the show was scheduled to start.

"Are you okay? I guess watching the world president get murdered by the man sitting next to you was a bit unsettling," Thadd said.

"I'm fine. You better get the show started." Josh didn't look up from his papers.

Thadd shuffled back to the box. "He's really distraught," he said to Eli.

"I've never known him to be concerned over someone's opinion before." Eli said. "I thought he laughed in the face of Emily Wells. Why would he let her upset him?"

"Don't know." Thadd cued Josh.

"Hi folks, welcome. It's the Josh Cohen Show, where the world waits to hear what I think. It's day 1,255 of the Jerusalem Covenant. Our phone number is 816510 if you'd like to be on the program today. Now," Josh paused. "I imagine most of you saw the horrible scene of World President, Christopher Heinman, dead on the floor at the Temple banquet last night. And," Josh paused again, "those in the United States also saw the scene of your president, Emily Wells, screaming at me. That's right, folks. Emily Wells believes I am to blame for the actions of a crazed rabbi. Also coming up today is news of the greatest evangelical revival yet to hit the earth, and a discovery of Jewish tribal records. Gotta take a break, folks. Don't go away."

Ariel checked her lipstick and hair in the rearview mirror before getting out of her car and walking the short distance to Josh's apartment. The moon lit her way, and crickets muffled the rapid click of her heels. Ariel stopped at his door and hesitated before knocking.

Will he think I'm too forward? she wondered.

She turned to leave when suddenly the door opened, as if Josh had known she was standing there.

"Ariel!"

"Oh, hi. I can't stay. I'm sorry, you were on your way out." She tried to back away but Josh reached over and put his arm around her, gently urging her inside.

"No, don't be silly. Come in. Sit down. Would you like something to drink? Wine?"

"Well..."

"What kind, white?"

"Yes, thank you." Her heart pounded. She sat down before her knees buckled. She smoothed her straight skirt and crossed her legs.

"Here you go." Josh admired her legs as he handed her the glass and settled in beside her.

"Thanks." She grasped the glass with both hands. She didn't want him to notice the quiver he caused.

"So what's up?" Josh enjoyed the smell of her perfume. "My father and I listened to the show today." She stared into the wine glass.

"What did you think?" Ariel's opinion meant more to him than almost anyone's.

"Well..." she wavered. "I'm worried about your safety."

"My safety. Come on, Ariel," he said, exasperated.

"My father is too, Josh." She hurried on, "We've talked about it. You're in the middle of something you can't understand." She put the wine glass down and stood up.

"You're wrong, Ariel. I do understand, and that's the problem. Christopher is not dead."

"You don't know what you're saying. Of course he's dead. He's lying in State. I've seen him. He is dead! His funeral will be covered live on every television network."

"No, Ariel. God!" he cried out, looking for the words to explain. He got up and paced the floor. "I've been reading Revelation, and I believe Christopher Heinman is the Antichrist."

"The what?" Ariel knit her brows. "Josh, what are you talking about? I've heard people speculate that he was the Messiah, but..."

"This is so hard to explain. You've just got to take my word for it. He is not dead. You'll see."

The time had come for Satan to be removed from heaven. For too long he had had access to the throne of God, accusing the brethren day and night. Michael searched him out and the confrontation began.

"There is no longer a place for you in heaven, Satan." Michael faced him with firm resolve.

"Come on, Michael." Satan smiled. "We were friends once. You don't really want me to go. I'm not that bad. I don't agree with God on everything, but I think we could work together again." Satan's demons snickered in the background.

"God has commanded, Satan. You will leave!"

For a short time, life on earth remained strangely dormant while the heavenly war raged. Unceremoniously thrown from heaven, Satan realized his doom was sealed.

"Woe to the earth, for Satan has come down to you, knowing he only has a short time," shouted the angels as the saints praised the name of Almighty God.

Pope Simon Peter looked forward to laying Christopher Heinman to rest. He smiled as the cardinal handed him his alb. *It'll be hot in full vestments, he mused, but I'd walk through hell itself to be rid of Christopher. How nice to never have to see his smug face again.*

Simon Peter looked regal as the procession walked the mile from the Temple, through the valley of Kidron, and up the western slope of the Mount of Olives to the burial ground. Millions across the globe viewed, close up, faces of the privileged, the leaders, the elite of the world government.

Ford Devoe escorted Emily as they made their way to the front to view the body. He didn't want any hard feelings until he could claim his rightful title.

Devoe gazed at the serene face of Christopher, nestled in the white plush lining of the casket. The fragrance of white orchids, roses, and lilies floated through the air. Even in death, Christopher radiated elegance.

Ford began to calculate his monetary loss. *On the other hand,* he comforted himself. *Christopher has become too popular. There can be only one world president.*

He smiled.

Ariel stood at the back with Josh, having turned down an invitation to sit with her father at the front. Her hand gripped Josh's arm. His words burned in her mind. "Christopher's not dead. Christopher's not dead." Perspiration loosened her sunglasses as the noon-day sun beat down on the crowd.

Pope Simon Peter opened the 'Book of Unity' and turned toward the congregation. He looked up and saw Emily's hand jerk to her mouth, her eyes wide with disbelief, focused behind him. Simon spun around, dropped his book, and stumbled backward.

"Do not fear, my friends," said Satan with the voice of Christopher Heinman. "I am alive. Three days ago I had a head wound. As you can see, I'm healed, and ready to usher in the new kingdom."

Simon Peter faltered, looking up as a vision appeared. He froze. Mary of Fatima hovered over Christopher, her arms outstretched.

"My son," she said.

The sky grew dark. The wind swept through the crowd with a chill. Women screamed as others fainted. Men wailed and tore at their clothing, while some shouted, "Messiah."

The pope fell to his knees and bowed his head. The crowd followed his example. Christopher savored the scene before him, until he met the strong, hazel eyes of Josh Cohen.

The atmosphere vibrated with tension. Josh grabbed Ariel's arm. "Come on." He pulled her away, down the hill toward the old city.

The wind swept around them, a sudden chill permeating the air. Sounds of adoration were heard coming from behind them as they fled.

Jerusalem went wild with the news of Christopher's resurrection. Cries of "Messiah" rang everywhere except at the Wailing Wall.

"Woe to the earth," the two old prophets shouted.

The world marveled at the amazing signs and wonders being displayed in the heavens. They gave all the glory to Christopher Heinman. The world eagerly awaited a global press conference scheduled once Christopher's doctor released him from the prescribed rest following his recent ordeal.

Christopher paced the floor of his office and glared at Simon. "I want you to get rid of those two madmen preaching doom and destruction. Their following is growing, and they're making a spectacle of me with their accursed miracles.

"And I'm plagued with complaints about the draught, the bloody water, boils, etc., etc. that those guys are bringing down on us. The people are begging for my protection and I intend to give it to them." Christopher pounded the desk, screaming, "I expect results! Do you understand?"

"One other thing." Christopher immediately cooled. "How's my statue coming?" He placed his hand on Simon's shoulder.

"Oh, it's finished." Simon became wary of Christopher's sudden change in personality. "We were going to place it at your tomb, but..." Simon avoided Christopher's eyes.

"Good!" Christopher rubbed his hands together. "I want it erected today."

"Where would you like it put?" Simon asked, arching his eyebrow.

"At the Temple, of course, in the Holy of Holies—where it belongs." Christopher began to bristle. "You saw the vision. Have you already forgotten who I am?"

"No, Lord. Forgive me. But the Jews are sacrificing in the Holy of Holies. I don't think they'll allow your statue to be..."

Christopher interrupted him in mid-sentence. "Did you not hear what I said? I want it in the Holy of Holies where it belongs!" His eyes were flashing and his whole body tensed up.

Simon backed up frightened. "I'll see that it is done immediately." He bowed and left the room.

He acts like a man possessed, Simon thought as he rushed down the hall.

"Greetings, friends and foes. Coming to you live from the city of miracles, it's the Josh Cohen Show. Today is day 1,260 of the Jerusalem Covenant." Josh's voice carried the confidence of one who knew the score. "If you haven't by now, it's time to pack your bags and flee to the mountains. But don't be disheartened. I think we'll get through today's show before you have to leave. Back in a minute."

Thadd and Eli couldn't believe what they were hearing. The phone lit up like the Temple menorah.

"Great," Thadd said. "We're going to be arrested for starting a stampede."

"What's worse," Eli added, "is that I'm wondering why we're still here?"

The commercial break ended and Josh raced back into the monologue.

"We're back, folks. My production people tell me that your calls of concern are flooding in. Let's go to the phones. Harry in Austin, Texas."

"I can't believe I got through. I've been listening to you for years," Harry blurted, suddenly becoming self-conscious.

"I'm glad you called. What's on your mind, Harry?"

"We're bailing out of here, too. It's bad everywhere. A dear friend of mine was murdered..." Harry fought to control his voice.

"I'm sorry, Harry. I've heard how bad the crime and violence have gotten in the U.S. Matter of fact, Israel's recently had record numbers of Jews immigrate, and a large number of them from my previous residence of New York City." Josh continued long enough for Harry to regain his composure.

Harry cleared his throat. "I've got a ranch, one of the few left that the government hasn't repossessed for a wildlife refuge. Several of us are leaving today. Food is becoming scarce. There's little economic activity, except in the government sector; and it's dangerous to even leave the house these days." Harry fought to keep back the thoughts of Sally.

"So, Harry, you and your friends are just going to ride it out in the wilderness?"

"Not exactly. The Bible tells of people who'll help the Jews during the 'great tribulation.' We believe our ministry will be just that. Hopefully we'll be set up to feed and provide some kind of shelter for people running from the Antichrist."

"Wow! Harry you're the first person who's told me how they'll ride out the coming tribulation. I wish you well, my friend."

"Thanks, Josh. You too!" Harry hung up the phone and wept.

13

"If the world hate you,
ye know that it hated me
before it hated you.
If ye were of the world,
the world would love its own;
but because ye are not of the world,
but I have chosen you out of the world,
therefore the world hateth you."
(John 15:18, 19)

The slaughtered bodies of the men *Time* magazine named "Prophets of Doom" remained in the street, ghoulishly illustrating the perversion the world craved. For three days their bloodied bodies headlined every newscast, and the earth celebrated their demise. In the midst of triumph, the festivities ended and the fun stopped.

The heavens opened and a voice like a trumpet called the prophets names. "Come to me. Your work is finished." Life was breathed into them, and they ascended in a cloud.

Their enemies looked on, trembling and gripped with fear. The earth moaned and cracked as the tectonic plates shifted for position.

Simon had elected to stay in Vatican City while the celebration around the dead prophets raged in Jerusalem.

"Your Holiness, are you all right?" The pope's devoted secretary burst into the office. "That was a bad one, at least an eight. I didn't think it would ever end." He picked his way through the damage left behind by the quake. "This place is a disaster."

"Yes, I'm okay." Simon Peter pulled himself out from under his desk.

"Do you think that was a sign from God about those two prophets?" the secretary asked innocently.

"No, I don't think that was a sign from God," the pope mimicked. "Get out of here."

The secretary scrambled to leave.

"Go check for damage," Simon yelled, slamming the door after him.

The cloud of dust that rose from collapsing buildings darkened the sky over Naples. Fires broke out and were then quenched by an eighty-foot tidal wave that pounded the shore, drowning the survivors who had not been buried or burned.

Across the world another major tremor sent the inhabitants of northern California scrambling for safety. Catastrophic events were now viewed as common occurrences.

In the state of Washington, Mt. Saint Helens rained down molten rock and debris. Ash drifted across the northern United States. Almost as if responding to a call to action, the volcano on the big island of Hawaii bellowed out in like response.

News magazines and wire services were no longer able to concentrate their attention on one disaster at a time. Reporters couldn't get to the scene of one tragedy before reports of another, even worse, followed on its heels.

Stan backed his car out of the garage, voicing a prayer of protection. The events of the last two days weighed heavily on his mind. Pictures of the gauntlet stretching from the first-floor booking room to the cells upstairs haunted his days. He couldn't block out the sounds of women screaming and children crying. Stan knew there had been a crackdown on believers. The SSS force had been enlarged to locate and bring in underground believers. Reward money had been upped, and calls poured in.

That last night on the job plagued Stan's dreams. He had just clocked out when the double-decked bus pulled in. Stan cringed at the thought of the atrocities going on behind the blacked-out windows, and knowing he could do nothing to change what was coming for those innocent prisoners. He watched as the doors slid open. Skinny, pitiful-looking people stumbled down the stairs, bleeding from the recent assault. Periodically the driver gave a shove to speed things up.

Stan had watched horrified as men, women, and children were stripped and forced up the stairs. SSS officers lined both sides of the stair well, shouting cat calls, obscenities, and vulgar threats.

"No!" Stan yelled at the memory, hating himself for not having been able to do something to stop the persecution of the saints.

Tommy opened the car door, breaking the spell, and Janet slid in beside Stan.

"You okay, Stan?" Janet asked, seeing the beads of sweat that dampened his forehead. They all knew the horrors that Stan had witnessed—the physical aspects of spiritual warfare that had Stan on the verge of a breakdown.

"I'm fine, thanks," he said, pushing aside her concern.

"We'll keep back a few blocks behind you." Tommy paused to get Stan's attention. "Harry's concerned it may draw attention if we travel together. You've got a map if we get separated." Tommy caught Stan's eye. "Whatever you do, don't stop for us."

"We'll make it, Tommy," Janet assured him. "You just keep Marilyn and Harry in line. I don't want to see any smooching in the backseat." She laughed.

"Come on, Janet," Stan chuckled.

Tommy smiled and shut the door. Walking to the car, his heart raced in contemplation of the long drive to Colorado and the possible dangers they faced getting there.

Leaving Austin, Marilyn watched the capitol building go by. Tommy and Harry talked in the front seat. As they approached the outskirts of town, an unbearable odor penetrated the car.

"Ugh, what is that smell?" Marilyn covered her nose.

"It's the city dump. I haven't been out here since I closed the restaurant, but I don't remember the smell being this bad,"

Tommy said. The smoke of several fires rose above the piles of garbage.

"Look at those dogs." Marilyn pointed to a pack of dogs stirring up the dust.

"What's that they're dragging?" she asked.

Tommy looked at Harry, both of them recognizing a mangled body. "I don't think we'll be here long enough to find out, Marilyn," he said as his foot pressed the accelerator.

Only half of the prisoners en route to the Detention Center in Arizona survived the accident. Kevin was greatly relieved that Donna escaped, but he feared for her whereabouts. The large camp had at first swallowed the small group, but as days went by, the camp population increased to over 1,000. Buses from around the western United States arrived daily, loaded with "criminals." Kevin quickly realized that the majority of prisoners consisted of believers.

Unlike the Nazi war camps Kevin had read about, this camp didn't include the fear and hopelessness. Bible study and prayer groups had formed, and praise services occupied the evenings.

The camp size grew as the world experienced the greatest evangelistic movement of all time. As a result of more prisoners, the food supply shrank and daily rations decreased. The children were served first, and then the women. Kevin went to bed hungry every night, yet satisfied with the words of the Lord: "I am the bread of life, he who comes to Me will never hunger, and he that believes on Me shall never thirst."

He often relived the bus crash and how he was jarred awake by the explosion. Occasionally he had to fight to overcome the guilt that assaulted him because he had been thrown safely away from the bus.

Praise God that Donna's away from here. Somewhere safe he hoped and prayed.

He was thankful that Donna hadn't been hurt and that Shirley had lived long enough to tell the story of how Donna mustered the strength to pull her out of the bus before it blew up.

What faced him and the believers in the camp who had recently studied the book of Revelation kept his mind occupied during the days.

One morning, several men decided to walk the perimeter of the camp.

"What exactly are we looking for, Kevin?" Mark Thomas, a new believer asked.

"We're looking for a way out of here." Kevin realized how little most of these people knew about the great tribulation.

"Should we have a lookout?" Sam Timmons asked.

"I don't think we need to. The guards rarely pay attention to us. This is probably the easiest job they've ever had. It's like Vacation Bible School here. Everybody's entertained." Kevin laughed.

"Why don't we just stay here where it's safe, until Jesus comes?" Jeff Carson suggested.

Kevin fought to control his emotions. Jeff had two beautiful little girls and his wife was expecting their third. His family rarely experienced hunger in the camp, and Jeff had closed his eyes to the hunger that others endured.

"Jeff, I don't mean to scare you, but we won't be allowed to just live here, peacefully, until Jesus comes. When Satan gets thrown from heaven, he'll come down with a vengeance against God's children," Kevin explained.

"I thought his anger would be against the Jews," Jeff said.

"Yes, that's true." Kevin took a deep breath. "But when he's unable to destroy the Jews, he'll turn to vent his wrath on all believers. Revelation 12:17 says, 'And the dragon was enraged with the woman, and he went to make war with the rest of her offspring, who keep the commandments of God and have the testimony of Jesus Christ.'"

"So," Jeff shuddered, "what will happen to us?"

"I don't know," Kevin said, grabbing Jeff with a hug and patting his shoulder, "but the Bible says we won't experience more than we are capable of bearing. Now let's go see if we can find a large hole in this fence."

Kevin quickly became the camp leader. Being one of the first camp prisoners, and because of his Bible knowledge, people with quarrels, questions, and fears eventually made their way to him. Even the guards used Kevin as a go-between.

The city of Brussels buzzed with activity surrounding the World Parliament Building open house. Every luxury known to man was at the beck-and-call of the attendees.

Devoe checked his tux in the mirror.

I should get in a weight program, he thought, looking at his small frame. *Just never seems to be enough time.*

He tossed that familiar thought aside and called down for his limousine. He looked forward to the tour of the new World Parliament building, one of the largest buildings in the world, covering four million square feet and costing over one billion dollars. Devoe almost envied Christopher his posh office on the thirteenth floor of the Berlaymont.

He owes it all to me, he thought, slicking his hair back. *It's time we start talking about my wants and needs.*

Emily tingled in anticipation of Christopher's open house. As Air Force One soared across the ocean to Brussels, she played one romantic scenario after another in her mind.

Refreshed by a short nap and soothing bath at the hotel, Emily slipped into her black strapless gown. She scrutinized her shapely image in the full-length beveled glass mirror and pictured Christopher standing beside her.

No man can resist me, she thought and blew a kiss to herself.

Simon Peter grudgingly accepted the few acknowledgments sent his way as he entered the lavish party suite.

You'd think all these people thought they were gods, he mused. *I don't think I like this turn of events. I'm entitled to their adoration.*

A scowl marred Simon Peter's face as he went to greet UN Secretary General Ford Devoe.

"Mr. Simon Peter, it's nice to see you." Devoe had little use for the pope or his religion.

"Mr. Secretary General," Simon Peter greeted him, noting Devoe's lack of respect for the papal office.

"I've been meaning to discuss with you what I'd like to do to honor our president." Devoe noticed the invisible wall that went up at the mention of Christopher.

"Oh?" Simon Peter took a step back and looked around the room.

"There's no one like Christopher. He's brilliantly solved the world's economic problems. He's brought peace to the earth. He's been raised from the dead. And if it weren't for those two horrid men in Jerusalem, our ecology would have been pristine by now. He deserves to be worshiped."

Simon Peter struggled to keep his composure.

I should want to worship him, he thought. *The blessed mother Mary appeared calling him son. But what about me*, he insisted to himself. *Where's my recognition? I'm the head of his church.*

Simon stared deep into Devoe's eyes. "What did you have in mind?"

"Some kind of symbol." Devoe studied Simon's jeweled cross.

"Like a cross?" Simon fingered the large diamonds.

"No, that's so barbaric. No offense." Devoe cleared his throat. "Christopher is a loving man, a gentle man. I suggest something that portrays the peace he's created, something like the peace symbol of the sixties." Devoe searched his mind for the right words. "Just think how much money the church could make with an exclusive right to sell the emblem." Devoe knew what buttons to push. "Not only that–everyone will want to have their own statue of Christopher."

Christopher showered Emily with compliments. He insisted she walk with him as he circulated among his guests. Emily was giddy. Even as the U.S. president she hadn't socialized in circles of royalty with kings and queens. It seemed that every other guest was a prince of this or that nation.

The evening progressed just as Emily hoped. It was obvious that Christopher was totally captivated by her charm and loveliness.

"Emily, let me get you a cold glass of champagne." Christopher took her glass.

"This one is fine, Christopher." Emily didn't want him to slip away, even for a minute. "Someone will be around shortly," she assured him.

"I'm headed that direction anyway. I insist." He took her glass.

Emily watched him leave the room as Devoe approached.

"Well, Emily, I see you've moved in." Devoe chuckled.

"Don't get in my way, Devoe. I know how to get what I want."

"Yeah, I know. Why else would you have stayed with your previous husband?" Devoe admired her cunning. "Just what do you plan to do about that ring on your left hand? You afraid Bob might suddenly reappear?"

She choked and looked down at her ring finger. "Don't worry," she said, clearing her throat. "I can fix it if I need to. The pope's a personal friend of mine," Emily taunted, raising her nose in the air.

Christopher returned with Emily's champagne. "So, Devoe, what do you think of our new building?"

"I'm impressed. And I don't impress easily." Devoe marveled at Christopher's magnetism. Not even a golden statue could adequately portray His Majesty.

"Come on, I'll give you and Emily a private tour." Christopher put his arm around Emily and led them to the glass elevator, using his key for the penthouse.

As the elevator soared to the top, Christopher caressed Emily's neck, and Devoe gazed out at the lights of Brussels. Emily melted under the touch, cursing Devoe's presence.

The doors parted and revealed Christopher's lavish tastes. Tropical flowers perfumed the air. Italian marble lined the walls and floor. Thick Persian rugs silenced the party's steps as the gold and crystal lighting softly lit the room. Emily's pulse throbbed. A burning flush raced through her body. Her eyes caught Christopher's, and she wet her lips.

Christopher dimmed the lights. "Devoe, there's champagne icing in the kitchen. Do you mind?" he said, reaching for Emily.

Devoe smiled. "Not at all."

"Emily," Christopher cooed as she moved closer, wrapping his fingers over the top of her dress.

Emily closed her eyes, then stumbled backward, feeling Christopher jerk on the delicate fabric. "Don't..." Her cry was silenced by the savage crushing of his lips, his body forcing her to the wall, making escape impossible.

Devoe chuckled in the kitchen. A deadly scream interrupted his thoughts. He hesitated...then poured just two glasses of champagne

14

"Behold, it is come,
and it is done, saith the Lord God;
this is the day whereof I have spoken."
(Ezekiel 39:8)

Greetings, oh ye who are persecuted. This is a special edition of the Josh Cohen Show. Evil has descended on the earth like a black shroud. Wars, strife, famines, pestilences, earthquakes, and falling stars rain around us. Does this seem bad? It is but the beginning. The trumpets are yet to sound, and God's wrath is yet to be poured out. The three woes, the worst of all plagues, will soon be announced. Don't go away. Back in a minute." Josh smiled at the horrified faces of his producer and call screener.

He gathered his newspaper headlines together, waiting for the next segment. He jerked his head up, startled by Ariel bursting through the door.

"Are you nuts?" Ariel shouted, rushing over to his table. "You can't tell the world evil has descended, and to get ready because the worst is yet to come. Are you trying to get thrown off the air in Israel, too?"

Josh loved the way her eyes flashed when she was upset. "I didn't know you were listening."

"Don't be ridiculous. Of course, I was listening."

The sight of her standing there with her hands on her hips caused Josh to chuckle. "Calm down, girl." He inhaled the beautiful picture she presented, knowing this might be the last opportunity. "I appreciate your concern for my well-being, Ariel, but my life is not my own. This is my purpose. I can't stop proclaiming the truth any more than you can stop being Jewish." Josh winked at Thadd in the sound box, knowing he and Eli were straining to hear every word. Thadd cued the next segment before Ariel could continue.

"I'm back, folks. If you'd like to be on the show today, the number is 816510. Now," Josh paused, "some of you, especially here in Jerusalem, are wondering what I'm talking about. You'll be on the phone in a minute telling me that Israel's king reigns from the Holy of Holies, never mind that the orthodox Jews have proclaimed him an abomination and are running for their lives. Israel, you'll tell me, has enjoyed peace with her neighbors for the last three and one-half years." Josh drummed his desk.

"Sure, you'll say, there's war in Korea, and Russia is ablaze with violence as Zhirinovsky moves his army through the Ukraine, Moldova, Slovakia, the Baltic Republics, and battles Germany for parts of Poland. China has moved to unify all of Asia. North and South Vietnam are fighting. Mexican nationals are rushing the borders of the United States to escape their own civil war, and South Africa is no longer a bother to the rest of the world because all its inhabitants are dead of war and starvation, and the mighty United States, now possessing a small divided military force, is no help to anyone.

"So, you'll tell me, things seem bad everywhere else, but Israel is at peace." Josh slammed his fist down on the table. Everyone in the studio jumped.

"Wake up you foolish people and hear the message of the Kingdom of Heaven, and I quote from Zechariah 14:1-9, 'Behold, the day of the Lord cometh, and thy spoil shall be divided in the midst of thee. For I will gather all nations against Jerusalem to battle; and the city shall be taken, and the houses rifled, and the women ravished; and half of the city shall go forth and fight against those nations, as when he fought in the day of battle. And his feet shall stand in that day upon the mount of Olives, which is before Jerusalem on the east, and toward the west, that there shall be a very great valley; and half of the mountain shall remove toward the north, and half of it toward the south.

"'And ye shall flee, like as ye fled from before the earthquake in the days of Uzziah king of Judah: and the Lord my God shall come, and all the saints with thee. And it shall come to pass in that day, that the light shall not be known to the Lord, not day, nor night: but it shall come to pass, that at evening time it shall be light. And it shall be in that day, that living waters shall go out from Jerusalem; half of them toward the former sea, and half of them toward the hinder sea: in summer and in winter shall it be. And the Lord shall be king over all the earth: in that day shall there be one Lord, and his name one.'

"Folks, listen to what I'm telling you. Christopher Heinman is not the Messiah. He's not Christ. He's not your savior. He cannot bring peace to the earth, and above all, do not take his mark. If you do, you're doomed. I've gotta take a break. Back in a minute." Josh slumped in his chair, out of breath from his tirade.

He glanced up at Thadd and Eli in the sound box.

Ariel walked over and put her hand on Josh's arm. "What must we do?"

Thadd and Eli came out. "What do we do, boss? How do we accept the real Messiah?"

Josh realized at that moment how much he had come to love these people. "You've got to believe that Jesus Christ is the Messiah. He died for your sins and mine. His blood covers the Holy Seat and makes atonement before a righteous and Holy Judge. He is coming as King of Kings and Lord of Lords. He will establish His kingdom here on earth. Those that endure unto the end shall be saved and will reign with Him."

The moment passed as UN soldiers burst through the studio door.

"This is a popular place today." Josh laughed as he stood up and put out his hands, ready for the cuffs.

Simon Peter approached the cemetery in front of the eastern gate. The clouds hid the stars. Simon stumbled over freshly disturbed dirt and let out a stream of profanity. Why couldn't Abduel just come to the embassy for his money? No one cares who killed those two doomsdayers. The world rejoiced and would have continued if that earthquake hadn't caused so much damage. Simon cursed again.

His skin began to crawl as a breeze whistled around the headstones. Tall shadows fell across his path. The moon and clouds fought for control of the sky. The sounds of night creatures sent a shiver up Simon's spine.

"This is ridiculous. I have no business being out here at four in the morning." Simon chastised himself. "Where is Abduel?" Simon leaned back against a large monument. A bulky flying object swooped past his face, leaving a putrid odor behind. Simon wrinkled his face in disgust and cursed again.

His long robes whipped in the wind and leaves floated down around him. A dog howled in the far distance and was answered by an eerie cry from his left. Simon quickly turned to look. Seeing nothing, he expelled his breath, unaware he'd stopped breathing. Glancing behind him, he shivered at the thought he was being observed. "Abduel," he croaked as he slapped at an gnat buzzing around his face.

Simon tried to focus his eyes and see through the heavy fog that had descended over the cemetery. He jumped, feeling something under his robe brush against his ankle. Looking down at the tall grass that covered the grave, he laughed at his jitters. *What's wrong with me*? he chided himself. *I am the pope.*

The air stilled and the silence became unnerving. Simon caressed his jewel-studded cross.

The ground below began to crumble, no longer capable of holding his weight. "What the..." Simon tried to steady himself, grabbing the head tone behind him. His terrifying scream echoed through the deserted cemetery. Frantically he tried to free his feet from the unknown grip that pulled him deeper and deeper into the depths of hell itself.

Grave robbers in the area scattered. Screams, though common to the area, still gave them a bone-chilling fear.

Christopher threw back his head and laughed. Burn in hell, Simon Peter. Burn in hell!

Stan and Janet headed for FM 183, avoiding as many major intersections as possible. Janet chatted about nothing important, hoping to take Stan's mind off the horrible actions he'd witnessed at the station.

As they approached the 183 cutoff, Stan caught a glimpse of a dark blue sedan two cars back. His heart pounded, and his palms slipped on the steering wheel.

Janet noticed his agitation. "What it is, Stan?" She started to turn around.

"Don't turn around. I'm not sure, but I think we're being followed." Pictures assaulted Stan's mind. He quickly shut and opened his eyes, attempting to focus on the road. He turned, praying the car would disappear. He looked in the rearview mirror, seeing the blue sedan make the corner. Stan forced himself to control his speed as he turned back to the left. He slightly accelerated and took the first right. Stan tightened his grip, seeing the dark sedan pull in behind him.

"Get down, and don't get up." He shoved Janet to the floorboard. His foot, trained by years of car chases, adjusted for speed as he rounded each corner.

"Hang on," he shouted, speeding through the intersection. Janet heard the blare of car horns and the muffled shouts of angry drivers.

The dark sedan threatened to overtake them. Stan accelerated, not seeing the Volvo entering the next intersection. He started to turn, but a large bus loomed before him.

Janet rolled forward as the brakes squealed in protest. The smell of burning tires crept through the floor. Darkness descended and peace, sweet peace, swept her away.

Marilyn fell asleep, praying for Stan and Janet's safe journey, and theirs as well. FM 183 stretched on for miles as the sun dipped below the horizon.

"Tommy, look." Harry pointed ahead to the left side of the road.

"Look at what, Harry? I can't see that far ahead." Tommy squinted to see what Harry pointed at.

"It's two people, Tommy. What are they doing way out here?" Harry gripped the back of the seat as Tommy slowed down. Marilyn sat up as Tommy pulled over and rolled down his window.

"Hi, folks, where you headed?" Tommy looked for any telltale signs that might warn him of danger.

"We don't know for sure, somewhere safe," the man answered.

The couple looked to be in their early twenties, ragged, but wearing clean clothes. *Probably students like Kevin and Donna,* Tommy thought, briefly agonizing over their imprisonment.

"Safe is what we're looking for, too. We're headed to Harry's place in Colorado. If you'd like, you're welcome to come with us," Tommy said.

The young man peered into the car. "You seem like nice people." He looked at his female companion. "It's up to you."

She smiled as they got in the back seat.

Months passed and their numbers increased. Kevin watched the growth, surprised at the relative peace they lived in. Even though the guards stayed to themselves, leaving the affairs of the camp to be attended to by those imprisoned, they had offered seeds when food stopped being supplied by the government.

Kevin woke one particular morning, a strange feeling, plaguing his mind as he went about the morning, attending to the camp business as usual. Around noon, he noticed a white UN military jeep park at the camp office and watched three men dressed in SSS uniforms go in.

"Who's in command here?" the tall one asked.

"What's this about?" the senior camp guard asked. " We haven't had notification of an inspection."

"This isn't an inspection. All these people have been found guilty of their crimes and sentenced to death."

"What!" cried the guards. "Death? What do you mean?"

"Don't get so excited. They'll die easy enough. You're just lucky we haven't had time to transport one of the new death machines out here. Cuts the head off neat and clean. Assures death every time." The SSS officers broke into laughter.

Kevin's worst fears proved valid when the three men, followed slowly by the camp guards, walked over the compound with AK-47s.

The head guard approached him with his eyes downcast. "I'm sorry, Kevin. You'll have to gather everyone in the yard."

Kevin fought to keep the tears back as he spread the word. He felt his heart being wrenched from his chest as he watched Jeff and his wife and three little girls walk out into the bright sun with the hundreds of others. He looked into the sky hoping for a sign from God, and instead heard the words of Habakkuk:

"Why dost thou shew me iniquity, and cause me to behold Agrievance? O Lord, revive thy work in the midst of the years, in the midst of the years, make known; in wrath remember mercy. Yet I will rejoice in the Lord, I will joy in the God of my salvation."

Gunfire exploded, and God's people began to fall. Shouts of prayer ascended into the heavens. Songs of praise overpowered the sounds of rapid gunfire. The smoke cleared and revealed hundreds and hundreds of bodies covering the ground.

The ground shook. An angel descended from the heavens and proclaimed in a loud voice, "Fear God and give glory to Him, for the hour of His judgment has come."

Josh spent an uneventful night in the Jerusalem jail. He had expected worse. He woke early and was taken to the World Government courtroom, now operating from the Temple. Christopher had moved the majority of his staff to Jerusalem, operating only a skeleton staff in Brussels.

This was the first time Josh had been inside the Temple. It was more magnificent than he'd imagined. He was led up the ten steps between forty-foot-tall twin bronze pillars. They entered the entrance porch, the first and smallest room in the Temple, leading to the main room. Josh marveled at the interior walls, elaborately carved cedar panels inlaid with ivory and gold. He was awestruck at the magnificent seven-branched menorah and the golden altar of incense. Lining the north and south walls were five tables, ten lamps and lamp stands, and various other implements of worship. The guard halted in front of a fabric veil shielding the wall and single door behind it. Josh closed his eyes for God's guidance, and His words came forth, "For I will give you a mouth and wisdom, which all your adversaries shall not be able to gainsay nor resist."

The guard grabbed Josh by the arm. "Come on, you bigot, hatemonger, spreader of lies. Prepare yourself to meet your god." Josh recoiled. Sitting upon a golden box, canopied by pure gold angels, with fifteen foot wingspans, sat Christopher Heinman. The people around him were bowing low before the altar.

"Your name precedes you, Josh Cohen." Christopher grinned, anticipating the challenge of breaking this man who was adored by many.

"As does yours, since the garden," Josh retorted, feeling the coldness of evil all around him.

"This is the second time you've stood before me. I think it's time you give me the honor I'm due." Christopher wondered what it would take to get Josh to his knees.

"There is only One worthy of honor and praise, Christopher." Josh stood firm, waiting for the blast of Satan's fury.

Christopher clenched his fists. "You know I have the power to keep you off the air; your voice never more to be heard by your adoring fans."

"My adoring fans, as you put it, no longer need my guiding truth. The angels will preach the Gospel of the kingdom in all the world, and then the end will come." Josh watched Christopher's face contort.

"I thought you might feel this way, so I brought along a little incentive." Christopher motioned to his guards.

Josh lunged as he watched them bring Ariel in. "Hold him!" Christopher yelled.

Ariel's limp body hung between the two guards. Josh flinched at each cut and bruise. He ached to cradle her in his arms, to brush the tangled hair from her face.

"Her life is in your hands, Josh. What will it be?"

Josh's eyes lingered on Ariel. Christopher smiled as he watched the turmoil play itself out on Josh's face.

Josh glared at Christopher. "The Lord says, 'Do not be afraid of those who kill the body and after that can do no more. But I will show you whom you should fear: Fear him who after the killing of the body, has power to throw you into hell.'"

Christopher leaped from his throne. "I am god. I demand your worship." He yanked the shining silver sword from the sheath at his waist. He grabbed Ariel and smashed her head down on the altar. Raising his sword, he glared at Josh. "Her head will be the sacrifice for your refusal to bow down before me, Josh Cohen."

Josh struggled against the men holding him. "Ariel," he screamed as Christopher heaved the sword down.

A loud rumble shook the walls, the floor buckled, and the ceiling broke from the rafters. Men, as if rag dolls, hurled through the air. The earth jarred from its axis, and the seas and oceans splashed out of their basins. Jerusalem split into three parts and the cities of the nations collapsed. Every island disappeared. The mountains crumbled. Hundred-pound meteorites fell from the sky. The stars fell to the earth, the sun turned black, and men cursed God. Terror descended on the earth as it stilled itself for the worst yet to come.

Ford Devoe received word of the destruction in Jerusalem. He could only hope that Josh Cohen got what was coming to him.

All communication with Jerusalem had been knocked out from the quake, and DSI engineers would be working overtime to get back online with their Jerusalem counterparts.

Devoe called an emergency meeting of his top security team. As he walked into the conference room he passed by his new secretary. He glanced over, thinking at first he saw Joyce. A pang of hope shot through his heart. He looked again and his heart sank. The dark cloud that had been his constant companion since Joyce disappeared returned.

"Okay, guys," Devoe began. "We've got a problem here. There's been another devastating earthquake in Israel. Christopher Heinman has not been heard from yet.

"Now, I'm sure he's okay, but our reconnaissance photos indicate that Russia is moving south, and China is moving west toward Israel.

"It doesn't look good. I'm afraid our friend Christopher has made some enemies. We've got to get our people out of there."

"But, boss, shouldn't we notify the Israeli government of the impending attack?" one of the younger engineers asked.

"Who are you? How long have you been around here, son? No, we're not going to notify anyone. We have contracts with Russia, China, and half the world. Do you think we're going to risk losing those clients over a no-win situation for Israel. Now get to work, all of you."

For three days Israel lay in ruins while rescue teams worked to dig out survivors.

The earth shook continuously while the people of the world shook their fists at God Almighty.

The whole ecological balance was disrupted. The sun did not refrain from blasting the earth with its intense heat. Then just as suddenly the sun went out and the world was plunged into darkness.

Satan gathered his forces to descend on Jerusalem and obliterate the opposing armies. The nations were united for the purpose of destroying the holy city—

The saints in heaven watched as "The seventh angel poured out his bowl into the air, and out of the temple came a loud voice from the throne, saying, 'It is done!'" (Rev. 16:17).

He woke with a start and sat up on the couch. He took a deep breath. *I must have dozed off. What time is it?* A beer commercial blared from the TV. His eyes glanced at the clock, 7:30. *Strange.* He brushed his hair back and stood up. His stomach felt empty and queasy. A few steps across the room and he was in the bedroom. The Bible lay open on his bed. His heart jumped and Harry raced to the phone and dialed Kaye's number. One ring, two rings, bile rose in his throat. Three rings. Someone would have answered by now. Four rings.

"Hello, this is Lee. Kaye and I are unable to come to the phone. At the beep, please leave a message and we'll return your call."

The sound of the beep caused a terrifying fear to squeeze his heart. He knew leaving a message would be useless. His call would never be returned. He lowered the receiver, then he heard something.

"Kaye?" He jerked the receiver back to his ear.

"Kaye? Kaye, is that you?" His voice shook.

"Hi, Harry. Sorry I couldn't get to the phone. I'm out of breath. We just got back from a walk. Did you feel that shaking? Do you think it was an earthquake?"

He sat down on the bed. His knees began to shake. "I'm gonna be sick."

"What's wrong? Do you need us to come over?"

Harry closed his eyes and rubbed his forehead. "We've got to talk. I thought the rapture happened."

"What? Harry, what are you talking about? We don't know when it will happen. It could be today, tomorrow or ten years from now."

He could hear the concern in her voice.

"I mean, I had a dream. It was terrible. Oh..." he rubbed his forehead again. "I don't know what happened to me. But I can't ever go through that again. I've got to know this Jesus of yours."

Harry hung the phone up. He fell to his knees and looked up.

"Almighty, God, can you hear me? It's me, your wayward son, Harry Levine. We haven't talked in a long time...I guess not since my Bar Mitzvah.

"Anyway, I've been away, in another world—I don't know, I've been blind, asleep, totally out of it—I've sinned against you. I've denied your Son. I've made a joke of His sacrifice for my sins—forgive me."

Harry broke down. Heavy sobs racked his body.

God called out to His Son, "It's time. Get them!"

Ministry Resources

Surprising as it may seem, it took years of searching to find some of these, my favorite ministries. With the release of this book, I wanted to make it easy for you to find them too. They are listed in no particular order.

FOR INFORMATION CONTACT:

Gary Bauer, President
Family Research Council
700 13th St., N.W., Suite 500
Washington, DC 20005
202-393-2100

American Family Assocation
Journal
P.O. Drawer 2440
Tupelo, Mississippi 38803

Insight
National Assocation of Evangelicals
450 Gundersen Dr.
Carol Stream, IL 60188

Torch
Texas Eagle Forum
P.O. Box 702098
Dallas, Texas 75370
972-250-0734

Dr. Tim LaHaye
Family Life Seminars
P.O. Box 2700
Washington, D.C. 20013-2700

Prophetic Observer
Southwest Radio Church
P.O. Box 1144
Oklahoma City, OK 73101
405-789-1222

Zion's Hope, Inc.
7676 Municipal Drive
Orlando, FL 32819
800-4-I-S-R-A-E-L

Gary H. Kah
Hope For The World
P.O. Box 899
Noblesville, Indiana 46061-0988
1-800-984-7883
Fax: 317-576-1053

Prophecy In The News
P.O. Box 7000
Oklahoma City, OK 73153
405-634-1234

Unravelling The New World Order
FAMC, Inc.
3500 JFK Parkway
Fort Collins, CO 80525
1-800-336-7000

Flashpoint
Living Truth Ministries
1708 Patterson Road
Austin, TX 78733
1-800-234-9673

Jews for Jesus
60 Haight Street
San Francisco, CA 94102-5895
http://www.jews-for-jesus.org

Grant Jeffrey Ministries
P.O. Box 129, Station "U"
Toronto, Ontario, M8Z 5M4
Canada
www.grantjeffrey.com/

i.e. issues and events
William T. James
P.O. Box 1108
Benton, AR 72018-1108

Personal UPDATE
Koinonia House
P.O. Box D
Coeur d'Alene, ID 83816-0347
1-800-546-8731

THM Journal
Take Heed Ministries
P.O. Box 350
Murraysville, PA 15668
1-412-327-2948
http://www.nb.net/~takeheed

Charles Crismier
Save America
P.O. Box 70879
Richmond, VA 23255
804-740-7775

Christian American
Christian Coalition
1801-L Sara Drive
Chesapeake, VA 23320
1-800-455-9900
http:/www.cc.org

David Barton
WallBuilder Report
P.O. Box 397
Aledo, TX 76008
817-441-6044

Here's Life San Antonio
Soapy Dollar
P.O. Box 12472
San Antonio, TX 78212
210-341-2442

Jack Van Impe Ministries
Box 7004
Troy, Michigan 48007
http:/www.jvim.com

Watchman Fellowship, Inc.
P.O. Box 13340
Arlington, TX 76094-0340
http:/www.rampages.onramp.net/
~watchman/

The McAlvany Intelligence Advisor
P.O. Box 84904
Phoenix, AZ 85071
1-800-528-0559

Precept Upon Precept
P.O. Box 182218
Chattanooga, TN 37422

Page 30 ("radical Christians")

They've got to be made to understand that intolerance is the root of all hate in the world.